For a mome ~~~ **s.**

He'd never had ~~~ But when Kaylee took another ~~~ looking as if she wanted to climb into his client's lap, instinct drove Max to move. He reached out, snagged Kaylee's hand and drew her toward him.

He could return her to her mother with some strong words about keeping the child out of his hair, as Jane had promised to do. Instead, he scooped Kaylee onto his knee. She looked up at him with big, questioning eyes, and Max prayed she wouldn't let loose with an earsplitting scream as she had the day before.

But after a moment or two she looked away and settled into his lap, shoving her thumb into her mouth.

Finally the meeting concluded, and Kaylee was fast asleep, drooling slightly on Max's shirt.

He had to admit it was a rather nice feeling, having a little girl trust him to this degree.

Dear Reader,

Everyone yearns to be part of a loving family, one
in which love is given and taken in equal measures,
where each person contributes, and each person has
a voice and is given respect. I'm so lucky to have been
born into a big, noisy, loving family in which I was
encouraged to grow and develop my talents, to be
whoever I wanted.

Not everyone is so lucky, however. In *The Good Father*,
I wanted to explore the feelings of characters who
have never been part of a warm and loving family.
They've had fleeting glimpses of it in their lives, but
they're both afraid to reach out for what they want,
lest they be disappointed yet again.

Of all the heroes and heroines in the SECOND SONS
trilogy, Max and Jane are probably the most complex.
What they show the outside world only scratches
the surface. I confess this book made me cry when I
wrote it (think Kathleen Turner at the beginning of
Romancing the Stone).

I hope you enjoy Max's and Jane's journeys toward
love and belonging. With this book, the Remington
cousins' story is complete. Their uncle Johnny, who
put everything in motion, would be proud.

Best,

Kara Lennox

The Good Father

KARA LENNOX

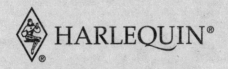

HARLEQUIN®

TORONTO • NEW YORK • LONDON
AMSTERDAM • PARIS • SYDNEY • HAMBURG
STOCKHOLM • ATHENS • TOKYO • MILAN • MADRID
PRAGUE • WARSAW • BUDAPEST • AUCKLAND

Recycling programs
for this product may
not exist in your area.

ISBN-13: 978-0-373-75260-7
ISBN-10:   0-373-75260-1

THE GOOD FATHER

Copyright © 2009 by Karen Leabo.

ABOUT THE AUTHOR

Texas native Kara Lennox has earned her living at various times as an art director, typesetter, textbook editor and reporter. She's worked in a boutique, a health club and an ad agency. She's been an antiques dealer and even a blackjack dealer. But no work has made her happier than writing romance novels. She has written more than fifty books.

When not writing, Kara indulges in an ever-changing array of hobbies. Her latest passions are bird-watching and long-distance bicycling. She loves to hear from readers; you can visit her Web page at www.karalennox.com.

Books by Kara Lennox

HARLEQUIN AMERICAN ROMANCE

Chapter One

Jane Selwyn's knees felt watery as she made her way across the steaming asphalt parking lot toward the three-story office building. The Remington Agency was her last chance for gainful employment in Port Clara. In the span of a few short weeks, she'd gone from pampered, rich man's wife to begging for a job from the man who had unwittingly broken up her marriage.

Not that the marriage hadn't already been gasping its dying breaths. But Max Remington's flirtations had finished it off in a hurry.

Jane stepped into the building's cool interior and checked her appearance one last time in the lobby mirror. She straightened the lapel of her red power suit and glossed on another layer of lipstick. Her silk blouse was already damp and sticking to her skin—August in South Texas was brutally hot, even on the coast. Still, she looked the part of a successful executive. Unfortunately, her pathetically slim portfolio told a different story.

For six years she had devoted her days to keeping

herself and her home beautiful for her husband and raising their daughter. Scott had freaked out whenever she even mentioned getting a job. But now it was just her and three-year-old Kaylee, and no money. Employment was a necessity.

Everyone said she was crazy to ask for so little in the divorce. But no one had known how desperate she'd been to get out with no one else hurt. Now she was the proud owner of a sleek cabin cruiser—her settlement—and a single mother of a gorgeous child, both of which ate away at her meager savings.

She never would have applied to the Remington Agency if she hadn't exhausted all other possibilities.

The agency was on the third floor of Port Clara's nicest office building. Jane paused before the door and sent up a prayer that Max would see past the humiliating events of their early acquaintance, past her short résumé, and give her a chance.

She straightened her spine and opened the door, then sucked in a breath of surprise. She hadn't expected a local ad agency to be quite so upscale. Though the reception area was small, it screamed class with its stone floor, rough limestone walls, and water cascading down a waterfall in the corner. With all the ferns and the muted lighting, she felt as if she'd entered a small corner of a rain forest.

A stylish woman of indeterminate age sat at a semicircular desk that looked as if it had erupted right from the stone floor. She smiled serenely at Jane.

"May I help you?"

"I'm Jane Selwyn. I have an interview with Mr. Remington at one o'clock."

The receptionist, whose nameplate said she was Carol Washington, looked at Jane with sympathetic brown eyes. "Didn't you get my message?"

Oh, no. Her cell phone had run out of juice just before lunch. Currently it was charging in her car. "I didn't check my voice mail," Jane stated without apology. "Is there a problem?"

"Mr. Remington had to run out—some type of printing emergency. He told me to extend his apologies."

"Oh." Jane almost sagged with disappointment. "Can I reschedule, then?"

"Actually, Mr. Remington has already made a decision about the artist."

"Without even interviewing all the candidates?"

Carol hesitated. "I'm sure he would look at your work as a courtesy."

A courtesy? Like hell. He'd caused her divorce, or at least accelerated the timeline. The least he could do was give her a shot at the position. "I'll just wait here until he returns."

"Why don't I make you another appointment," Carol said smoothly.

So he could cancel that one, too? "I'd prefer to wait." She was going to see Max Remington today, one way or another.

Carol nodded just as a door opened behind her and Max Remington appeared. "Carol, has John Canfield—" Surprise registered on his handsome face as he spotted Jane and recognized her. "Jane? What are you doing here?"

"I'm here to interview for the artist position."

"*You're* Jane Selwyn? I thought your last name was Simone."

Jane inhaled sharply. He was even better-looking than she remembered. After a few months in Port Clara he'd acquired a golden tan, and his unruly hair had turned more blond than brown.

He wore neatly pressed jeans riding low on his slim hips and an open-collar shirt, no tie, no jacket, and she felt ridiculously overdressed. Few people wore suits in their laid-back beach community, but she'd thought it appropriate for an interview.

Fortunately, he didn't seem to mind. In fact, his lingering gaze said he approved, but not in a completely professional way.

Her face flushed. She told herself it was the weather.

"I changed back to my maiden name." She'd wanted nothing to remind her of Scott.

"I told Ms. Selwyn that the job was already filled," Carol put in.

Max quickly overcame his surprise and smiled, revealing even, white teeth. "It's great to see you again."

Jane stood, fumbling her portfolio before she could extend her hand to accept his warm handshake. "I'm surprised you would make a decision without interviewing all of the candidates."

"Well, now, I was leaning toward one applicant, but I haven't made a final, final decision yet."

Carol peered at him skeptically over her half-moon reading glasses.

"Why don't you come back to my office," Max continued. "Pardon the mess—the workers are still putting in the finishing touches."

Mess was right. Men were laying carpet in the hallway, painting walls, installing light fixtures. Jane had to dodge ladders, sawhorses and paint buckets, and once she nearly tripped because her attention was focused on her potential employer's buns.

She'd sworn up and down to her ex-husband that she hadn't been flirting with Max that fateful day of their first meeting a few months ago. But he'd certainly been flirting with her, and on some level she had responded to him. How could she not? How could any woman with a pulse not feel drawn to such a gorgeous male?

He held the door of his office open, and she entered. It was large but not ridiculously so and a little bit messy, but nothing like the hallway outside. At least it had carpet, paint and furniture.

He cleared off a small table and pulled out a chair for her. "Sorry to be so casual. My conference room furniture hasn't arrived yet."

"This is fine. You're certainly doing up everything first-class." She settled into the chair, again juggling her purse and portfolio. Why did she feel so awkward? As a corporate wife she'd been required to handle all kinds of social situations, from formal banquets to funerals to ladies' coffee klatches, and she'd never had problems saying the right thing or fitting in. But now she second-guessed every word.

"Advertising is all about image." He settled at the table across from her and placed her résumé, such as it was, in front of him.

"Your reception area certainly makes a statement."

"You think it's too much?" He sounded a bit worried.

Goodness, why would he care what she thought? "No, I think it's lovely. I love the sound of moving water."

"I guess you would, since you live on a boat."

She wished he didn't know quite so much about her already. But his cousin, Cooper, owned the fishing charter boat berthed next door to her, and she was close friends with Cooper's wife, Allie. In fact, she and Max had both been in Cooper and Allie's wedding, though they'd hardly exchanged two words. She'd been very subdued that day, wanting to feel happy for her friend but unable to shake her overall pessimism regarding marriage.

In addition to her living situation, Max also knew she was freshly divorced and a single mother—and that her millionaire ex-husband had a violent temper.

"Why don't I show you my portfolio?" Jane said brightly, wanting to get it over with. She figured her work would speak for itself. Either he would see her talent and give her a chance, or he wouldn't.

She unzipped the large, black leather case, a thoughtful graduation present from her parents, and opened it in front of Max. He flipped through it silently, scrutinizing each page.

"I'm not familiar with any of your clients. Can you tell me a little bit about them?"

"They're mostly fictitious," she blurted out.

"Excuse me?"

"Most of this work was done as class assignments. The businesses don't exist. Remington Charters is the only real client I've ever had." She had designed a logo for Allie's fishing business before Cooper had come on the scene.

She expelled a long breath. There, she'd gotten the worst news out.

"Your résumé says you've been working freelance since you graduated."

"A gross exaggeration to get me in the door," she admitted. "If you want the absolute truth, I don't have much experience. But I have talent, education and technical know-how."

"Can you do video computer editing?"

She nodded firmly. "I did some video work in school. I'm sure the technology has advanced, but I can learn it. I'll learn it on my own time."

He looked at her, at her artwork, then back at her. He was going to reject her, that was obvious.

She leaned forward slightly. "Just give me a chance, Mr. Remington…Max. I won't lie to you. I need this job. I'm already behind on my payments to the marina, and pretty soon they're going to kick me out and…and I'll just have to drift, I guess."

Oh, God, she hadn't meant to say all that. *Please, sir, I want some more.* Could she humiliate herself any further?

Max studied the woman sitting across from him. He'd been surprised as hell to find out *she* was Jane Selwyn. If he'd known, he never would have even scheduled an interview.

But now that she was here, he felt obligated to at least consider her for the position. After all, she'd gotten dressed up in that Queen Elizabeth suit for the occasion.

The first time he'd met her, she'd looked quite different. She'd been wearing a bikini, in fact. And what a bikini. Sure, bikinis were pretty much par for the course in Port Clara, but Jane wore hers better than any other he'd seen. In fact, he'd like to see—

He gritted his teeth. Best not to dwell on what she looked like under that suit. He tried desperately to think like a businessman.

Hiring Jane Selwyn would be illogical. He'd already interviewed a better-qualified candidate who was perfect. But though Carol was right that he'd made a decision, he hadn't yet contacted the artist to offer the job.

He could still reconsider.

Jane's portfolio showed talent, but it was decidedly amateurish. And despite the small-town atmosphere of Port Clara, he had no intentions of limiting his services to local used-car dealers and barbecue joints. He intended to compete with agencies from Houston—New York and San Francisco, too. Jane was *so* underqualified.

But the biggest reason of all not to hire her was what she did to him on a physical level. He'd never met a more beautiful woman. Not just your average beautiful, like a model or a beach bunny, but an ethereal, angelic beautiful. With her black, wavy hair, her high forehead and her lush red lips, she reminded him of one of those 1940s movie stars—Vivien Leigh, maybe.

Her husband had been right to punch Max in the face. Although he hadn't made any outrageous come-ons when he'd first met her, his thoughts had been decidedly carnal, and good ol' Scott had sensed it.

Max had been in the business world long enough to know that work and sex mixed together like nitro and glycerin. Workplace affairs caused no end of heartache, not to mention the loss of productivity. If he hired Jane, their relationship would have to be strictly business.

Of course, he'd decided long ago he would never act on his attraction—the minute he'd seen her darling, bright-eyed, blond-haired little girl.

Single moms were off-limits for Max. He didn't need that lesson shoved down his throat again.

"I'll work for free," she said, breaking into his thoughts.

"Excuse me?"

"Give me a two-week trial, and you won't have to pay me. We can call it an internship. Let me prove what I can do. I'll work twice as hard as anybody you could possibly find. I won't complain. I'll take work home with me at night. I'll…I'll…" She trailed off as she apparently ran out of incentives.

Thank God she hadn't offered fringe benefits with the boss, or he might have snapped up her offer.

As it was, he couldn't help but consider what she had proposed. The one problem with the other artist was the salary he'd demanded. Launching this business had been far more expensive than Max had planned for. His cousin Reece, who was also his CPA, was having kittens over the cost overruns for the office remodeling. Getting free graphic arts services would help with his bottom line.

But he quickly nixed the idea. It wouldn't be fair to Jane. She obviously needed a job, which meant she needed money, too. She had mouths to feed.

And he had to hire the best-qualified candidate.

Max stood, signaling an end to the interview. "It was a pleasure seeing you again, Jane. As I said, I haven't made a final decision yet, but I'll let you—"

"You aren't going to hire me, are you?"

"I'm still considering all—"

"My ex-husband and I finalized our divorce because of you," she said abruptly. "You owe me."

He hadn't seen that coming. Cheeky move. "Oh, really? I thought I did you a favor."

"No, actually, I did *you* a favor. If I hadn't agreed to Scott's rotten divorce terms, he was going to claim you and I had an affair and drag your name through the mud. He said he would ruin you and your business here in Port Clara before you even got started. And he could, believe me."

Max sat back down with a thud. "I remember he made some threats, but I thought that was just heat-of-the-moment stuff. Did he actually think we were involved? Based on one conversation?"

Jane nodded. "He thought I was having affairs with everyone, from his brother to the pool boy. But in you, he found someone he could actually damage. And not just with his fists. He knew where you came from, all about your family. He could have caused you considerable embarrassment with his lies, if nothing else."

"Why didn't you let him? You barely know me. He couldn't have proved anything."

She blew out a breath and massaged her temples with two well-manicured fingers. "You seemed like a nice guy. You didn't deserve to have Scott as an enemy. He wouldn't have been able to prove anything, but by the time we went to court, the damage would have been done."

They sat silently for a few moments. She was right— he did owe her. Still…

"I can't believe I just did that," Jane said finally. "Trying to force your hand. It was something Scott would do. Please, forget I even brought this up." She stood and gathered her things. "I don't want to be hired if I'm not the best qualified."

"Wait a minute, Jane—"

"No, really, it's okay. This never would have worked out, not with this history between us. I shouldn't have even sent my résumé in. I'll see myself out."

She fled his office, and he let her go before he said or did anything he'd regret. He watched the way her hips moved when she walked, the little hitch that said she was only the hottest woman he'd ever met in his life. But he couldn't think about that, he had to think about the big picture.

He felt sorry for her, he really did. She was obviously in dire straits if she would resort to using guilt to get him to hire her.

She had talent—lots of talent. She needed the job, which meant she would work hard to please Max and his clients. Her salary demands as outlined in her résumé were modest, unlike those of the candidate he'd been leaning toward.

Max took a sip from his coffee cup and grimaced when he realized it was left over from this morning and stone cold.

Had he really been a factor in Jane's divorce? Allie was tight-lipped where Jane was concerned. But she'd given him the impression that Jane's marriage had been on the rocks long before Max's ill-fated flirtation that had resulted in a black eye and a fat lip.

Max sauntered into the reception area, where Carol presided over their only coffeepot. He'd ordered another one for the office break room, but it hadn't yet arrived.

"What in the world did you do to that girl?" Carol asked. "She flew out of here like her hair was on fire."

"We have a history," Max said, hoping that would end the matter, but of course it didn't. Carol always wanted to know everything that was going on and she had an unhealthy interest in Max's love life. But she was very good at her job, juggling phone calls and packages, soothing ruffled feathers and keeping all those plants alive. She was a keeper, even if she was a tad nosy.

Carol removed her reading glasses and arched one

well-plucked eyebrow at him. "I gathered that. I guess you aren't going to hire her."

"Actually…I'm thinking about it."

"Mm-mm, Mr. Remington, are you letting your hormones make decisions for you? I'll admit Jane Selwyn is a beautiful woman, but—"

"She's very talented. And she needs the job." That was something Carol should understand. She was recently divorced, too, and she hadn't been the most qualified candidate, either. But he'd followed his instincts and hired her. His instincts seldom led him astray.

So what were his instincts telling him about Jane?

The jury was still out.

"Thank you so much for looking after Kaylee," Jane told her friend Sara, who happened to be married to Reece Remington, another of Max's cousins. Port Clara had experienced something of a Remington invasion back in the spring, when the three cousins had inherited the fishing business from their uncle.

Jane thought it rather peculiar that two of her best friends were now married to Remingtons, but they all seemed so happy. Around them, she always tried to reflect back that happily-ever-after feeling they both radiated.

"I'll watch her any time." Sara still held on to Jane's three-year-old and seemed reluctant to turn her loose. "She's so good. Plus, when I have my own kid I'm hoping you'll return the favor." Sara patted her tummy, though her pregnancy didn't show at all yet.

Jane sighed and sank into one of the overstuffed

chairs at the Sunsetter Bed-and-Breakfast, which Sara and Reece had recently bought. "How much could I make as a babysitter in Port Clara? That may be all that's left for me."

"So the interview didn't go well?"

"It went about as badly as an interview can go. To start with, Max has already made a hiring decision. He saw me out of courtesy, probably because of my association with Allie and Cooper. But I lost it. I acted like a harpy. I told him he owed me because it was his fault…" She stopped abruptly, not wishing to talk about Scott or the divorce in front of Kaylee. Her daughter, almost four, was growing bigger and smarter every day. She was a sponge, soaking up everything she heard and often repeating it.

Sara understood anyway, and her eyes widened. "Jane, you didn't."

"It just came out of my mouth."

"It wasn't really Max's fault…was it?"

"No. Scott and I were attempting a reconciliation that weekend, but it never would have worked. If it hadn't been that incident, it would have been another.

"I know it's all for the best. But that doesn't change the fact that I need work and I just blew my last chance."

"You know," Sara said cautiously as she disentangled Kaylee's grasping hands from her long, curly brown hair, "I could ask Reece to put in a good word—"

"No, please. This whole thing has been humiliating enough. I'm an intelligent, responsible adult with a college education. I should be able to get a job based on that. I refuse to use connections to get what I want. That's too much like…well, you know."

Sara sank into her own chair, shifting Kaylee onto her lap. "I was so sure that job would work out for you. You're exactly what Max needs. Are you positive there's no chance?"

"Max wouldn't hire me if hell froze over." She paused, then said something she'd only toyed with before today. "I'll have to sell the boat."

"Oh, no. You *love* the *Princess II*."

"It's an extravagance, and I can't even sail it without help. If I sold it, I would have enough money to tide me over until I get on my feet."

Jane's cell phone rang and she immediately perked up, hoping it might be another job lead. She'd dropped résumés all over town, and even a few in Corpus Christi, though the larger city was almost an hour's drive from Port Clara.

"Jane Selwyn."

"Jane, it's Max Remington. The job is yours if you want it."

Chapter Two

By eleven o'clock on Jane's first day of work at the Remington Agency, she was terrified Max would fire her before lunch.

She hadn't been all that strong in computer skills at school, and what little she'd learned was woefully out-of-date. Her first assignment was to lay out a simple ad for a new restaurant. Max had given her everything she needed—copy, photo and graphics. She could see the ad in her mind. But getting the computer program to do her bidding was an effort in frustration. So far she'd spent more time reading the manual than actually getting anything done.

She had finally figured out how to size her photo and adjust the color balance when Max tapped on her partially open office door and stuck his head in.

"Is the ad done yet?"

"Um, no, not quite yet. When do you need it?"

"Five o'clock today."

"Okay."

"Want me to pick up lunch for you?"

"Sure, that would be wonderful." It was a cinch she wouldn't have time to go out to eat. She would be lucky to get this sucker done before she had to leave at 2:45 to pick up Kaylee from preschool.

She had arranged for an after-school babysitter, but Mrs. Billingsly couldn't start until next week. Jane had explained about her shortened workdays to Max, who hadn't taken the news with a smile. He probably already regretted hiring her.

Jane reached for her purse in her desk drawer, intending to give Max some money, but he waved it away. "I'll take care of it. But you will get the ad done, won't you?"

"I'm doing my best."

Max flashed a strained smile. "Great."

Jane returned her attention to the screen and yelped in surprise. Her photo had turned green. The people looked like Martians. She must have hit the Okay button by mistake when she was adjusting the color balance.

She held her breath and hit Control-Z, the panacea for undoing mistakes, and thankfully the photo turned back to its normal colors.

Jane worked steadily, making slow progress and glancing worriedly at the clock.

By 2:45 she had everything roughed in like she wanted it—but she needed to make some refinements. Now that she was getting the hang of it, she found the graphics program to be incredibly powerful. She could certainly be finished by five—if she didn't have to pick up Kaylee.

She grabbed her purse and attempted to slip out of

the office unnoticed, but as luck would have it, Max came into the hallway just as she did.

"Oh, Jane. Are you done with the ad?"

"Um, almost. I have to pick up Kaylee. But I'm coming back, and I'll finish up before five, for sure." She turned away from him and headed for the exit.

"Wait. You're bringing your daughter here?"

Jane turned back slowly. "That was the plan."

"Jane, this is a place of business. It's not a day-care center."

"This is an unusual situation. Once I have my baby-sitter, this won't be a problem. I did explain that to you, right?"

"Yes, but that was before I knew you would take all day to do an ad that should have taken you a couple of hours."

"I haven't been wasting time, really. Most of today was spent learning the program. Anyway, I only need a few more minutes to finish up, and Kaylee won't cause any problems, I promise." She mentally crossed her fingers. Kaylee was very well behaved most of the time. But every so often she still threw a hideous tantrum, a holdover from the Terrible Twos. *Just please, don't let it be today.*

He tried again. "The office isn't a safe place for a child."

"She'll be fine. I'll keep her with me in my office. You won't know she's here."

Max clearly wasn't happy about the arrangements, but he didn't argue further. "The ad will be done by five? And you'll e-mail it to me?"

"Absolutely."

Finally he relaxed his stance. "All right."

"I really have to go or I'll be late. They charge extra if I'm late picking up, and I can't afford it."

"Do you need an advance on your salary?" he asked suddenly. "'Cause if you need money for food or something—"

"That's not necessary," she said quickly. "I'm okay." She hurried away, pondering the Jekyll-and-Hyde routine. First Max was Simon Legree, then he was Mother Teresa.

She was a bit surprised at his hard-nosed attitude regarding children. The corporation where Scott worked as a marketing manager featured its own day-care center and liberal policies for working parents. She knew Max's company was tiny by comparison, but his attitude seemed antiquated.

Well, some people were simply uncomfortable around children, she reasoned. That was something to keep firmly in mind whenever her heart did its annoying little pitter-pat in his presence.

Yes, he'd done her a huge favor by hiring her. But that was no reason to feel anything but professional toward him.

Kaylee was cranky when Jane picked her up from the private Montessori school, which Jane's mother had offered to pay for. Her mother had warned her that if she divorced Scott, she shouldn't expect to move back home and live off her parents' largesse, not that Jane would have considered that. But when Jane had told her mother about her new job, Wanda Selwyn had tut-tutted about young children needing their mothers, then had offered to pay tuition if Jane would enroll Kaylee in the best preschool available.

"Just because you've made some foolish decisions, that's no reason your child should suffer," Wanda had proclaimed. Wanda wasn't so much upset about the divorce as she was about the settlement her daughter had accepted. Jane hadn't confided her reasons for bowing to Scott's unreasonable demands.

Jane had been willing to listen to a sermon or two if it solved some of her child-care problems. Though Max hadn't taken her up on her offer to work for free, her starting salary wasn't much more than she could have earned as a waitress. But he'd promised her raises would be forthcoming once she proved herself.

"I don't like that place," Kaylee proclaimed as Jane buckled her into her car seat.

"Really? What don't you like?"

"Icky food."

"Maybe you'll like tomorrow's lunch better. Is that all?"

"Billy took my bunny. He's *mean*."

"Oh." Jane slid behind the steering wheel, wondering what the appropriate advice was. Should she encourage Kaylee to share? Or was this mean boy a bully, someone Kaylee should stand up to? Lord knew she wanted to teach her daughter to be independent and learn to solve her own problems.

Jane's parents had not raised her to be independent. They had raised her to be a rich man's wife. Looking back at her marriage with some hindsight, she now knew she had been drawn to the security Scott offered her. She had convinced herself she was in love with the handsome but overbearing man, and she had mistaken Scott's possessiveness for love.

Truth was, she didn't really know what love was, only that her and Scott's relationship had been unhealthy from the start. But she had been too scared to leave him, too scared to try to make it on her own. It was only when his behavior began to border on abusive that she'd filed for divorce—before he could carry out any of his threats.

"Macaroni for dinner, Mommy?" Kaylee asked, the bunny incident apparently forgotten.

"Absolutely. But first I have to finish some work at my new job."

"What's a job?"

"You know. Like Daddy goes to work every day to his job. Now I have a job. I…draw pictures, and I get paid money for them."

Kaylee frowned. Her father's long working hours had been a continual source of friction in their family. Maybe Kaylee believed her mother would stay away all the time, too. No doubt about it, Jane's job would require a lot of adjustments. Kaylee was used to having almost constant access to her mother.

"I'll be going to my job every day to work," Jane said. "But I'll be home every night for dinner. We'll still play together and I'll tuck you in and read you a story every night."

Kaylee still looked worried. She was growing so fast, getting more complex every day. Jane usually had no idea what was going on behind her daughter's bright blue eyes. The child had taken her parents' breakup reasonably well. Not having her father around wasn't much different than before the divorce, as Scott had spent very little time at home. He had either been working, playing golf or dragging Jane around to this party or that while Kaylee stayed home with a sitter.

Once parked at the office building, Jane grabbed a tote bag filled with favored toys, unbuckled Kaylee from her car seat and walked with her inside the cool lobby.

Carol looked surprised to see the child, but then her face melted into a smile. "What an adorable little girl!"

"This is my daughter, Kaylee," Jane said. "Kaylee, this is Ms. Washington."

Kaylee held out her favorite yellow baby blanket, now tattered and faded. "This is my blankie."

"And a very nice blankie it is, too," Carol said.

"My after-school child care doesn't start until next week," Jane said, then lowered her voice. "Is Mr. Remington here?"

"No, he's out calling on clients."

"Oh." She was actually relieved. Bringing her daughter to the office on her very first day was unprofessional and she knew it. But she simply didn't have a choice in the matter.

"Did you need something?" Carol asked.

"No. I just have a tiny bit of work to finish up, and I thought he'd be here to approve it before I left for the day."

"Oh, don't worry. If he doesn't like something, you'll hear about it."

"Really?" From what Allie had said—and what little Jane had previously observed—she thought Max was the easygoing, laid-back Remington cousin. He'd been somewhat testy with her earlier, but she'd attributed that to anxiety over his deadline.

"Don't get me wrong, he's a good boss," Carol said. "I mean, I've only been working for him a short time, but he's fair-minded and flexible. You always know exactly what he wants from you, so you aren't expected to read his mind like with some bosses.

"But he does want things a certain way, and he's not shy about telling you."

"You mean he's a perfectionist?"

"Yeah." Carol nodded. "That's a fair description. But not in a nitpicky way. You'll see what I mean."

"Mommy." Kaylee tugged on the hem of Jane's skirt. "Can I get a drink?" She pointed to the gurgling fountain.

Oh, Lord, she could just imagine Max returning to the office and finding Kaylee with her head in his fountain.

Carol grinned. "We have some juice in the break room. You want me to watch her while you work?"

"Oh, would you? That would be great."

"You come with Aunt Carol," Carol said to Kaylee, standing and holding out her hand. "We'll see if we can find juice and a yummy snack in the break room." Carol looked at Jane. "Is that okay?"

"Sure. I'll only be a few minutes."

Jane hurried to her office, listening for sounds of Kaylee's displeasure at being abandoned. But she seemed to take to Carol, which wasn't surprising; Kaylee wasn't a clingy, shy child and usually was happy to meet new people.

As Jane worked on the ad, making only small adjustments now and feeling slightly more confident with her graphics program, she could hear her daughter's happy but shrill voice and laughter coming from the break room down the hall.

When the ad was as good as Jane knew how to make it, she e-mailed it to Max as per instructions. She looked at her watch, surprised that it was nearly five o'clock. That had taken far longer than she'd expected. Time flew by so quickly when she was engrossed in something creative.

Thank God for Carol. If Jane had been forced to divide her time between her computer and entertaining Kaylee, she never would have made the deadline.

Jane found her purse and headed out of her office, grateful she had survived her first day of work. Just as she closed her door, she heard Max's voice and froze, torn. Part of her wanted to see him and have him look at the ad. His approval was important to her on this, her first assignment. But another part of her wanted to make a clean getaway. Max was exciting to be around, but a little draining on her, too. She was ready to share mac-and-cheese with her daughter and decompress.

"Who's that?" she heard Max ask.

Oh, no. He was in the break room with Carol and Kaylee.

"This is Jane's daughter, Kaylee. Kaylee, can you say hi to Mr. Remington?"

If Kaylee said anything, it was too quiet for Jane to hear.

"I'm watching her while Jane finishes up some work."

"And don't you have work to do? What if a client arrives? Is anyone answering the phone?" He sounded decidedly grouchy.

Darn, Jane hadn't meant to get Carol in trouble.

"I can hear the door chime and the phone from here," Carol said, not sounding at all bothered by Max's reprimand. Then again, she was probably a good ten years older than Max and seemed pretty sure of herself.

"Well, I hope this isn't going to be a regular thing. Having a child running around the office isn't the kind of image I'm trying to project."

Carol grumbled something Jane couldn't make out.

"Did she at least finish the ad she's been working on?"

"I don't know."

Jane decided she'd done enough skulking around in the hallway, eavesdropping. She strode toward the break room and entered boldly. "Oh, hello, Max. I hadn't realized you were back."

"Mommy!" Kaylee, who'd been scribbling in a coloring book, flew out of her chair and attached herself to Jane's leg.

Jane leaned down to pick up her little girl. "Have you been a good girl for Ms. Washington?"

Kaylee nodded. "We ate Goldfish and juice—"

"And some apple slices," Carol interjected, probably so Jane would know the snack had been somewhat nutritious.

"—and we played horsey and colored in the book—"

"Excuse me," Max said, looking more and more irritated, "but can we finish our business before you're off in MommyLand?"

"Yes, of course, Max. What is it?"

"Is the ad done? Please tell me it's done."

"Of course it's done," she said calmly, as if she'd finished it ages ago. "It should be in your inbox as we speak."

He bolted out of the room.

"He's mean, Mommy." *Mean* must have been Kaylee's new word.

Carol laughed. "Not mean. Just not into kids, I don't think. Listen, you better hit the road before Mr. Remington looks at that ad and decides he wants changes."

"Oh, but it's perfect," Jane said, alarmed to think she might have more work to do. "I'm sure he'll be pleased with it." The finished product had been beautiful, even if she did say so herself.

"One thing you better learn fast in this business, honey. No matter how hard you work, no matter how perfect it is when you let go of it, the boss will always want changes and the client will, too. The sooner you realize that and don't let it bother you, the better."

Jane nodded. "Point taken." She quickly gathered up Kaylee's toys and stuffed them into the tote bag. "C'mon, princess. Let's go home and have some macaroni."

They'd almost cleared the reception area when Jane heard her name. She considered scooting out the door and pretending she hadn't heard. But since Max had bellowed at her loudly enough to shake the walls, she decided she better obey the summons.

She sighed. Oh, God, what if he hated the ad?

He appeared in the doorway to the reception room just as she reached to open it. "Oh, there you are. I thought I'd missed you."

"Is something wrong?"

"Not much, really. The ad is beautiful. Really, Jane, you have such an eye for color and composition. There's just one teeny-tiny problem."

"What?"

"You left off the client's logo."

Chapter Three

Jane gasped. In the span of two heartbeats she'd gone from glowing with pride to cringing with mortification. She'd left off the client's logo? How could that be possible?

Just then Kaylee let out an unexpected shriek—right in Jane's ear. She strengthened her grip around Jane's neck, putting her in a wrestler's stranglehold.

"That man is *mean!*"

"What?" Max asked. "Did she just say I was mean?"

But Jane's mind was shifting back to the ad and the final steps she'd taken, and she remembered something. "I think I know what the problem is. Give me five minutes."

She dropped everything but Kaylee and ran back to her office. "Kaylee, honey, please be good for another couple of minutes while Mommy fixes this *disaster.*" How humiliating would it have been to show the client an ad with no logo?

While her computer booted up, she tried to convince Kaylee to play quietly, but the child was crabby now and wanted none of it. Jane had to work with Kaylee in her lap and Max standing in the doorway, glowering at her.

If she didn't fix this problem in two seconds, she was fired. She knew it.

She called up the file from the graphics program. Yes, there it was! She'd made the logo transparent while she was working on the background, and she'd simply forgotten to restore it. One button click, and the problem was fixed. With a huge sigh of relief, she sent it to Max.

"It's fine now. The corrected version should be in your inbox."

He didn't rush to his office, as she'd expected, but continued standing in her doorway staring at her, an inscrutable expression on his handsome face.

Oh, God. He was going to fire her anyway.

He opened his mouth to say something, then seemed to think better of it and turned away.

Jane wanted to get herself and her fussy child out of there—before the day got any worse. But she forced herself to wait until Max had okayed the ad. If he wanted her to do more work on it, she would, but she would find a babysitter first.

At least Kaylee had stopped crying. She was now flopped across Jane's shoulder, her little body relaxing muscle by muscle as drowsiness took over. Poor thing, today had been long and confusing for her.

Still carrying her daughter, Jane tiptoed to Max's office. He was at the computer, but he must have sensed her presence because he looked up.

"Is it okay now?" she asked.

"It's fine. I've sent it to the client."

"Do I still have a job?"

He actually smiled. "Yes, you still have a job. I shouldn't have reacted like I did, not on your first day. I'm sure things will go smoother once you settle in."

Jane smiled back. "Absolutely. See you tomorrow, then." She turned to leave.

"Oh, Jane. One more thing."

Shoot, what now?

"I'm courting a new client, a children's clothing manufacturer from Houston. If I land the account, it will be by far my biggest." He pointed to a folder sitting on the corner of his desk. "That's some of the print advertising they've done over the past couple of years, along with some concepts I've brainstormed. Would you mind looking them over tonight? I'll want you to do some mock-ups for a presentation. We can talk about it tomorrow."

"Sure, of course." What sort of mock-up was he talking about? Sketches, or something more polished? She should ask, but she didn't want to look any more ignorant today than she already had.

Jane grabbed the folder, which she would study after Kaylee was in bed. "Have a great evening." Did he have a date? Oh, Lord, why did she care about that? He could have ten dates, and it was none of her concern.

As she made her way to her car, the day's events floated around in her brain, but the one she focused on was when Max had said her ad was beautiful. Maybe his praise hadn't been sincere, but she'd gone all tingly inside.

For a moment, she imagined how it would feel to hear him say *she* was beautiful. The tingly feeling returned. It was a miracle she got her car home in one piece.

OLD SALT'S BAR & GRILL was nothing like the ultra-hip clubs in SoHo and the Village Max used to frequent when he lived in New York. But it had its good points— like a big deck that looked out over the ocean, decent food and drinks that didn't cost your whole paycheck.

Although lots of bars dotted Port Clara's coast and downtown area, Max and his cousins had adopted Old Salt's as their home away from home.

Max worked long hours these days trying to get the agency up and running and profitable—profitable being the point that interested him most at the moment. He had walked out on his job at Remington Industries, his family's New York conglomerate, with a lot of big promises about how he was going to make it on his own with no help from them.

He remembered how his older brother, Eddie, had stared at him slack-jawed, and his father—vice president of marketing—had clenched his jaw in anger, then declared Max would come crawling back before six months was out.

He'd thought their reactions kind of amusing back then. Now he didn't.

By eight o'clock Max felt worn thin, and he decided

to call it a night and head for Old Salt's for a beer and some commiseration.

He found the whole gang there—Cooper and Allie, unwinding after a full-day charter on their boat, the *Dragonfly;* and Reece and Sara, relaxing after a long day running their various businesses—between them they had three.

"Max!" Allie greeted him with a quick kiss to the cheek. "How goes the advertising biz?"

"A bit grueling today," he admitted as he swiveled a chair around and straddled it. The waitress caught his eye, and he pointed to Cooper's beer. She nodded.

"It's not easy, running your own company," said Sara. "The B and B isn't so bad, since I took over an already-thriving business. But the catering…all I can say is, I'm glad Reece has some business sense or I'd be in serious trouble." She put a hand to Max's shoulder. "How's the new artist working out?"

"Oh, you know about that?"

"Of course. I was there when you called her to offer the job. She's incredible, isn't she?"

"Incredible…yeah, that's one word to describe her." *Slow* would be another word.

"You're not pleased with her work?" Allie asked, reading between the lines. "Oh, Max, please don't fire her. She really needs that job. You have no idea what a financial mess Scott left her in. That boat was supposed to be hers free and clear, and now she's discovered all kinds of debts and expenses related to the boat she knew nothing about. Of course, Scott kept her totally in the dark about their finances—"

Cooper clamped a hand over his wife's mouth to silence her tirade. "Allie. Perhaps Jane doesn't want her personal life bandied about in public."

"We're not public," Allie objected, flipping her long red hair over one shoulder. "We're Jane's friends. Everybody here knows what a jerk her ex is. Max experienced it firsthand. First fist, that is."

Max rubbed his jaw, which was even now, months later, a little tender. He couldn't argue that Scott was a bastard, all right. Not only had the guy sucker-punched Max, but he'd used Max as leverage to take advantage of Jane in their divorce.

"The fact Jane needs a job shouldn't be a factor in whether Max keeps her on or not," Reece pointed out. He was the accountant in the family, the hard-nosed one who kept the rest of them financially on track.

"So he should just cast her out into the street?" Sara asked, with a look bordering on outrage.

"No, of course not," Reece said. "But you can't expect him to keep her on the payroll if she's not an asset to his business."

"Whoa, whoa." Max decided the discussion had gotten way out of hand. "I never said she isn't working out. Our first day was…rocky. Jane isn't accustomed to the fast pace in advertising. But I plan to give her a decent chance to adjust."

"I hope you're not bombarding her with criticism," Allie said. "She's very sensitive."

"But you have to give her feedback or she won't improve," Reece pointed out.

"Um, I gave her plenty of feedback." Max had actually been a bit harsh, which wasn't like him. He'd always had an easy-come, easy-go attitude when it came to winning and losing. Back when he'd worked at Remington Industries, if he spent weeks working with the creative staff on a campaign, only to have his father or Eddie or some other corporate suit shoot it down, he'd shrugged and moved on.

But now *his* money, *his* time, *his* reputation were on the line. His future depended on whether he could make a go of the Remington Agency. Eddie and his dad were watching, waiting for him to stumble and fail.

The situation made him tense, like a snake ready to strike. If he didn't take things a little easier, he would end up like Reece had been before he resigned his high-powered position and relocated to Port Clara—headed for a heart attack like his old man.

"What about the other factor?" Cooper asked, giving Max a knowing look. "Doesn't the fact you're hot for her get in the way of business?"

Max groaned. "Come on, Coop, don't bring that up. Yes, she's a beautiful woman, but I *think* I can manage to resist her. I don't need a harassment suit slapped on me, thanks very much. Besides," he added, "she's a single mom, and you know my rule."

Sara looked at him quizzically. "What rule?"

"Max doesn't date women with children," Reece supplied, seeming amused by his wife's narrowed gaze aimed at Max.

"That's horrible!" Sara said. "Are you telling me you

don't like children?" She turned to Reece. "He is *not* going to be the godfather of our first child."

Sara was expecting her and Reece's first, and she was a little prickly where babies were concerned.

"I never said I don't like children," Max objected. "There are other issues."

"Like a single mom can't shower all her attention on you," Allie said. "She has other priorities besides partying."

"What is this, Pick-On-Max Night?" Max took a long sip of his beer. "I came here for good company, not to have my life dissected."

Allie at least looked a little penitent. "Sorry, Max. Who else can we pick on?"

"You've already picked on me enough for one night," Cooper said. "I'll be glad when you all get tired of telling anyone who'll listen how I tried to get Allie arrested for stealing her own boat."

"And I don't want to hear any more seasick jokes," Reece put in.

"Or anything about my numbers dyslexia," Sara added. "Hey, you know I found out there's a term for my problem? It's called dyscalcula—a math-learning disability."

They continued to banter, but Max didn't take part. He was nervous as hell about his meeting with the children's clothing manufacturer he'd told Jane about. The owner of Kidz'n'Stuff was arriving for a meet and greet tomorrow, and Max was counting on Jane to come up with some sketches that would wow them, based on his concepts.

If she was as slow at sketching as she was with computer graphics, he was in serious trouble.

WHEN MAX ARRIVED at work the next morning, he found Jane already there, working industriously at her drawing board. She was prompt in the mornings, he'd give her that.

He tapped on her office door, which she'd left open as usual. "Morning, Jane."

She jumped and turned, smiling. "Oh, good morning."

"You don't look so good," Max blurted out, but her appearance was slightly alarming. Yesterday her coal-black hair had been curled and arranged in shimmering waves falling over her shoulders, and her makeup had been magazine perfect. Today she wore an untidy ponytail. What was worse, she had dark shadows under her eyes. And she wore glasses.

Was she trying to ugly herself up so she wouldn't tempt him? Had she sensed his nearly overwhelming desire for her? He thought he'd kept it pretty well under wraps.

He had news for her. Nothing she could do would make her ugly. But her lack of polish was such a contrast from the day before, he was afraid something was wrong.

Jane looked down at herself, then back up. "I guess I should have looked in the mirror before I left home this morning." She sounded embarrassed. "I lost track of the time and I got rushed. But I was so excited. Kaylee has a bunch of Kidz'n'Stuff clothes, and we both love them. I started just doing some sketches and, well, before I knew it the sun was coming up."

Max stepped into Jane's office. "You stayed up all night?"

"I didn't mean to. It's just that when I get involved in creating something, I lose track of time."

Finally he chanced a look at her drawing board, and his jaw dropped. "That's…that's gorgeous."

"Really?"

"Yeah, really." Jane had taken his scribbled notes and stick-figure drawings and turned them into a comp for a full-page magazine ad. But this was no rough sketch. She'd made drawings of two children that were so realistic they almost walked off the page.

One of those kids, he realized, was her daughter. The other was a little boy he didn't recognize.

"I used photos of Kaylee and a neighbor boy from Houston just as examples," she said almost apologetically. "I hope that's okay."

"Okay?" It was fantastic. Given the ridiculously short timeline, he hadn't expected anything this elaborate from Jane. "I thought we'd discuss concepts this morning and you could knock out a few rough sketches to show the client. But this—"

"I did too much."

"Well, yes. You really should have discussed this with me before you invested so much time, just to be sure we were on the right track."

"I know that now. But I wasn't thinking about it at the time. I'm just so excited to be using my art. For years I haven't been able to devote any time to it, and I hadn't realized it, but I…I'd shut down a part of myself.

And now I have that part back and…well, I'm sure you don't want to hear all that."

Actually, he was fascinated. It seemed that the beautiful, polished woman who had first attracted him was far more interesting than he would have guessed. Now he saw, in full color, the passion that lurked below her slick surface.

And it turned him on.

He wasn't sure how he felt about her revealing something so personal to him. It indicated a level of trust he certainly hadn't earned.

"I still have the rest of the day," she said, suddenly all business. "What changes would you like me to make?"

"Nothing. You nailed it." He didn't often feel that way about his artists' work. Usually there was a lot of back-and-forth before he was satisfied.

"How about this one, then?" She placed a second comp on the drawing board, and Max's jaw dropped yet again. It was another beautifully rendered drawing, showing the same little boy and girl, but in different poses. The first ad was "Tough'n'Sweet," one of his preliminary ideas for an ad campaign. This one was "Love'n'Play," which Jane must have come up with on her own. It showed the little boy getting a hug, and the little girl coming down a slide.

Max didn't know what to say. He'd seen that Jane had talent, but this was incredible. "Have you ever shown your work?"

She raised startled eyebrows. "Shown? As in, at an art show or gallery?" She laughed. "Other than in college, no."

"You could, you know. You're good enough."

"You aren't saying that because you're going to fire me, are you? Suggesting an alternative career to soften the blow?"

"No." He smiled, wanting to reassure her. "The second ad is good, too. You're going to work out here just fine."

She beamed at him, and his heart lurched unexpectedly. "Thanks."

"Why don't you go home and get some sleep? Sounds like you put in a full day of work before you even got here."

"Thanks, but I couldn't. They're doing some construction work at the marina right by my boat, and it's so loud I couldn't possibly sleep there during the day."

"All right. Hey, there's a couch in my office. Why don't you sack out there? I'm interviewing potential account executives this morning, so I'll be in the conference room where I won't bother you."

She looked at her watch. "You don't have more work for me?"

"I have a hot project coming in this afternoon, probably around one o'clock, but nothing more right now."

"A little nap, maybe," she conceded, then picked up one of her pastels. "Just let me put a few finishing touches on—"

"No." He stood and took the crayon out of her hand, instantly aware where their fingers briefly brushed. Though she might be slightly unkempt this morning, she smelled fantastic. "You'll get engrossed in your work and suddenly you'll look up and hours will have passed. If you want to fiddle with the drawings after your nap, fine, but they're perfect as is."

He ushered Jane into his office and cleared a stack of magazines and some mail off the sofa. "I've cat-napped on this sofa myself, so I can vouch for its comfort."

"Would you wake me up in an hour or so? I should be good to go by then."

"Sure." He drew the shades, turned out the lights and left her there. But as he conducted his interviews, his mind kept wandering to the sleeping beauty in his office.

She was something else.

After the second interview, he realized he'd left the third candidate's résumé on his desk, and he wanted to review it before the woman arrived. He opened his office door as quietly as he could and tiptoed in without turning on the light.

Jane was flopped on the sofa facedown, one delicate arm bent over her head, her dark hair spilling across her shoulders. Her slow, even breathing told him she was still dead asleep.

She'd wanted to be awakened in an hour, but he didn't have the heart to disturb her. He stood there for a few moments, watching and listening to her breathe. Then she rolled over, still asleep, her pale blue T-shirt riding up high and offering him a glimpse of her creamy stomach. Her navel peeked out over the top of her low-riding jeans. She had a tiny gold ring in it.

Funny, he wouldn't have thought Jane Selwyn to be

the type to sport a piercing. Maybe it represented her own little rebellion against the corporate-wife role she'd played during her marriage. The thought made Max smile as he slipped out and quietly closed the door.

JANE'S PHONE DREW HER out of a deep, deep sleep and she realized she'd done more than catnap. She sat up and tried to locate her cell.

There it was, on the floor. She bent and picked it up, seeing with a start that it was Kaylee's school. She became instantly alert.

"Jane Selwyn." Her heart thundered in her ears.

"Hi, Jane, this is Monica Wagner, the nurse at Kaylee's school. Now, don't worry," she said hastily, "Kaylee's okay, but she is running a low fever. She's complaining of an earache. You'll have to come pick her up. As you know, it's school policy that any child with a fever must be sent home."

Jane sighed. "I'll be right there."

She looked at her watch. It was after eleven—she'd slept for nearly three hours. It was enough that she could have worked the rest of the day with no problem, except for this little wrinkle.

Kaylee had experienced earaches before. She would have to visit the doctor and get an antibiotic. But where did that leave Max's hot project?

For the second day in a row, she risked arousing her boss's wrath and getting herself fired. But it was worse today than yesterday. Now, she had a taste of what this job would be like. She knew what she would be giving up.

The first ad had been a bit troublesome, but she'd begun to feel the power of the computer program by the time she'd finished. And the previous night had been incredible.

She loved this job. And despite his perfectionism, she loved Max as a boss. He was so passionate about his work, and his mere presence electrified her. She'd never wanted to please anyone as much as she did him, and that included her ex-husband.

She didn't stop to analyze what that might mean, or exactly how far she'd go to make him happy.

Chapter Four

"Wow." Ellen Lowenstein, owner and CEO of Kidz'n'Stuff, smiled in obvious surprise and pleasure as she studied Jane's drawings. She and Max sat in the newly furnished conference room, kicking around Max's ideas for an ad campaign. The carpeting had been laid yesterday afternoon, and the furniture had arrived only this morning.

Carol had literally been hanging the last picture when the potential clients had arrived.

Ellen was in her forties, round and matronly with salt-and-pepper hair and a penchant for dangly earrings. She was cheerful and upbeat, and Max felt he was making a good impression on her.

Unfortunately, also present was the Kidz'n'Stuff marketing manager, a hard-nosed, nonsmiling man with the unfortunate name of Ogden Purcell. It was hard to know what Ogden was thinking, because his poker face offered up no clues. But Max got a distinct impression the man would not be impressed with flash. He would want hard figures.

"I understood today was simply a get-to-know-you meeting," Ellen said. "I had no idea you would put in so much work on spec."

Ogden cleared his throat. "You do understand, Mr. Remington, that we're still considering several agencies."

"Yes, of course," Max said smoothly. "But my artist was so enthusiastic about the possibility of working on this account, she stayed up all night working on these. She really loves her work."

"It shows."

"Let's talk about print placement," Ogden said. "You said in your original proposal you had some fresh ideas?"

"Yes, I do." Max whipped out some documents he'd prepared for this moment. "I've been researching some smaller publications that are on the rise in terms of circulation. In my opinion, these lesser-known magazines…"

Max realized he'd lost Ellen. Her gaze wasn't on the numbers in front of her, but on something behind Max. Max turned, and his heart sank. A drowsy little girl had just pushed the conference-room door open and toddled into the room.

"My goodness, who is this?" Ellen asked.

Max wasn't sure if she was pleased or appalled to see a child roaming around the Remington Agency. "That's Kaylee. She has an earache and couldn't go to preschool today, so she's hanging out with us."

"She's the little girl in the ad!" Ellen said.

Kaylee stared up at Ellen, apparently fascinated with her bright colors and dangly earrings.

For a moment, Max was paralyzed. He'd never had to deal with a situation like this. But when Kaylee took another step forward, looking like she wanted to climb into his client's lap, instinct drove Max to move. He reached out, snagged Kaylee's hand, and drew her toward him instead.

He could pick the girl up and return her to her mother with some strong words about keeping the child out of his hair, as Jane had promised to do. But he hated to break up the rhythm of this meeting any more than it already was.

Instead, he scooped up Kaylee and placed her in his lap. She looked up at him with big, questioning eyes, and Max prayed that she didn't let loose with an earsplitting scream like she'd done yesterday afternoon, before her medicine had taken effect and dulled the pain of her earache.

He also hoped she didn't call him "mean" as she'd done two days ago. Having Ellen see him reviled by a little girl wouldn't help with his image.

But either Kaylee was too drowsy on medicine to show much of a reaction, or she had revised her opinion of Max, because after a moment or two she looked away and settled into his lap, shoving her thumb into her mouth.

"Anyway," Max said, "I've done some research into the demographics of some smaller circulation magazines…" He continued the presentation as if nothing was wrong, keeping one arm around Kaylee and using the other to point out the various numbers as he talked about them.

Ogden seemed interested. He asked several intelligent questions about the magazines, and Max answered them with confidence.

Ellen, however, seemed a little bored, and her gaze frequently strayed to Kaylee. Maybe numbers weren't her thing. Since she was the ultimate decision-maker, he tried not to get too technical.

She probably thought having a child at their meeting was the height of nonprofessionalism. If Jane and her wayward three-year-old lost him this account, he was *not* going to be happy.

Finally the meeting concluded, and Kaylee had fallen asleep, drooling slightly on Max's shirt. Wonderful.

Max stood as his potential clients did, managing to hold Kaylee with one hand and shake hands with the other. Kaylee didn't wake. She was a limp rag doll in his arms.

He had to admit it was a rather nice feeling, having a little human being trust him to this degree. She reminded him painfully of Hannah, the only other child he'd ever held like this, and his heart lurched at the thought.

Breaking up with Hannah's mother had been a relief. But losing Hannah—God, it would kill him to go through something like that again.

Max walked his clients down the hall. They took the beautiful ads Jane had drawn with them, intending to show them to others on staff.

"We'll be making a decision in the next couple of weeks," Ellen said. "But I'm very impressed by what I see."

Yesss! Max mentally punched his fist into the air. Kaylee hadn't blown it for him after all.

They'd almost made it to the reception area when the door to Jane's office burst open and she flew out, a panicked look on her face.

"Max! Max, have you seen Kaylee?" she yelled, looking a bit deranged.

He turned, so she could see Kaylee was safe and sound. "Shhh. She's right here."

"Oh, thank God." Jane rushed toward them. "I am so sorry. Last time I checked, she was napping on the pallet I made up for her, and then I looked over and she was gone—"

"Jane, it's okay."

"I hope she didn't ruin your meeting."

"On the contrary," Ellen said with a smile, "she was a welcome distraction from all the facts and figures. And it's so refreshing to see a man so comfortable with children."

Jane didn't bother to hide the surprised look on her face, but at least she didn't contradict the client.

"I'm Ellen Lowenstein." She held out her hand to Jane, who shook it, recovering her composure.

"It's so nice to meet you. I love your clothes. I mean, the clothes you design. Well, of course, I like your clothes, too. That's a lovely suit."

Max shot Jane a strong look, hoping she would just close her mouth. She was blathering.

"Thank you," Ellen said as Ogden stood mutely by her side, arms folded, not smiling. "Has Kaylee done much modeling?"

"Modeling?" Jane looked confused for a moment, but

then she got it. "Oh, you saw the drawings. No, I did those drawings from some snapshots, nothing professional."

"So you're the artist. It's doubly nice to meet you."

"Thanks."

Ogden pointedly looked at his watch. "We do have another appointment this afternoon."

"Right." Ellen smiled at the man. "Ogden keeps me on schedule. Well, you'll be hearing from us."

Max handed off Kaylee to Jane and walked his maybe-clients to the door.

"Do you like baseball?" Ellen asked suddenly.

"Yeah, sure," Max responded. "Although I have to confess, I'm still a Mets fan."

"We have a box at the Minute Maid Park. Perhaps you'd like to be our guests next week at an Astros game. With your wife and little girl, of course."

What? Ellen thought Kaylee was his daughter, and Jane his wife? He knew what he should do. He should immediately correct her misconception. But what came out of his mouth was,

"Sounds wonderful. We'd love to."

JANE JOGGED BACK to her office and gently placed Kaylee back on her pallet. The child didn't wake up. She'd had a miserable night last night, and consequently Jane had, too. They were both in desperate need of sleep.

Apparently, though, the antibiotics had finally kicked in. Jane only wished that when Kaylee had awakened, she hadn't wandered into the last place she ought to be.

Max was going to fire Jane. What choice did he have? She had promised to keep an eye on Kaylee and make sure she didn't bother Max, and Jane had broken that promise. Now the most important meeting in the Remington Agency's history had been compromised.

Jane headed back out of her office, stopped, returned to her desk, opened the bottom drawer and pulled her Klean-Up towelettes out of her purse. Then she scurried to the reception room, where Max and Carol were engaged in a spirited discussion.

"You are in so much trouble," Carol was saying.

Uh-oh. That didn't sound good.

"I couldn't help it. I got carried away in the moment. She liked me and I didn't want to burst her bubble."

"How are you going to explain this to Jane?" Carol asked.

"Shh. I'll think of something."

He'd already hired someone to replace her. That must be what they were talking about.

She burst into the reception area. "Max, I am so sorry." She tore open the foil packet. "I was focusing on the new ad, and I guess Kaylee woke up and crept out of the office without me seeing her."

She pulled the moist towelette from the packet and began attacking the drool stain on Max's chest. He wore a beautiful shirt with a pale olive pinstripe. It probably cost a month's salary—her salary, anyway.

Max jumped back. "What are you doing?"

"Taking care of that stain before it sets." Maybe she shouldn't have touched him without asking, but with a three-year-old around all the time she was used to jumping on stains, whether they were on her, Kaylee or someone else. "These little cloths are pretreated with stain remover. They work really well, even on oil and crayon. Spit should be no problem."

"Except this is a silk-blend shirt."

Oops.

He held out his hand. "Here, let me see it. I guess it couldn't get any worse." He took the towelette from her and scrubbed at the already damp spot on his chest.

"It'll look better when it dries." Well, duh.

She was normally a composed woman. Even in divorce court she hadn't lost it. Everything she'd said had been cool and confident. But around Max, she was a blithering idiot. Those people from Kidz'n'Stuff probably thought he hired mentally challenged employees.

"Oh, Max, I'm so sorry. I don't know what to say."

"It's just a shirt."

"No, I mean, about Kaylee interrupting your important meeting. What did she do?"

"She just wandered in. I picked her up and put her in my lap and kept going like it was an everyday occurrence."

Jane winced. "She didn't object?"

"Maybe it's the medicine she's taking, but she seems to not be repulsed by me anymore."

"You didn't repulse her," Jane objected. "She just met you on a bad day under bad circumstances. She generally likes everybody." Except maybe Billy the bunny-snatching bully. "But that's beside the point. Was the meeting ruined?"

"Actually, no. As it turns out, Ellen Lowenstein loves kids, and she was impressed we had a 'kid-friendly' office."

"Oh. So it actually…worked in your favor?"

"This time. But, Jane—"

"I know, I know. This isn't really a kid-friendly office, and I can't continue to bring Kaylee in to work. But she should be able to return to school tomorrow. Or the next day at the latest."

"You can't bring her back here," he said in no uncertain terms. "She's an accident waiting to happen. I've got work crews coming in later today, and tomorrow, too. She could get hurt, not to mention exposed to the wrong people—"

"I understand. I'll take her home, and I'll try to find a sitter. That is, if I still have a job."

"I'm not firing you," he said, his voice gentle now. "If I ever fire you, you'll know it."

Jane nodded, afraid to speak. She'd once again dodged the unemployment bullet, but only just. She dashed back to her office before Max could change his mind.

Carol gave Max an arch look. "You were kind of tough on her."

"Was I? I didn't mean to be. I had to stress the point, that's all. Kaylee *could* get hurt."

"Kaylee probably helped you land that account," Carol shot back, though she lowered her voice. "Ellen

Lowenstein is gaga over the child, and she thinks you're her father. You should be thanking Jane, not reprimanding her."

"I didn't reprimand her." He balled up the towelette, now dry, and tossed it in the wastebasket. "And I haven't won the account yet. Not by a long shot. Ellen might have been charmed by a child running around the office, but Ogden Purcell clearly wasn't. For all we know, he's the real decision-maker."

"The account is yours," Carol declared. "I could see it in her eyes. She adores you."

"Yeah, but that could all change if she finds out I'm not a family man after all."

"Hmm, now what are you going to do about that?"

Max got the distinct impression Carol was enjoying his predicament. "I'm not going to mention it again, that's all. If I have any more meetings with Kidz'n'Stuff, we'll do it at their offices in Houston."

"What about the baseball game?"

"Ellen probably wasn't serious about that," he reasoned. "If I don't mention it again, it'll probably be forgotten."

"Uh-huh."

IT HAD TAKEN SOME DOING, but Jane had arranged for babysitters the following day. Sara couldn't do it; she was busy catering some women's club luncheon. Allie was free in the morning, but she had a fishing charter after lunch. So she had agreed to run Kaylee over to the bed-and-breakfast at noon, where Reece, who ran his accounting business out of the B and B, had agreed to look after the child until Sara got home around three.

At least Jane wouldn't have to worry. Her friends would take good care of Kaylee. But just making the arrangements had been exhausting. She'd never before appreciated how hard it was to be a working single mom.

She arrived at the office a little later than usual, having spent extra time organizing Kaylee's medicine and explaining everything to Allie, who would in turn have to explain things to Reece. Then Kaylee had gone through a minimeltdown.

But it was still before nine.

Carol was at her desk, and two workmen were busy setting up an aquarium in the reception area.

"Oh, this'll be fun," Jane said. "Kaylee loves fish. Of course, I won't be bringing Kaylee in here anymore," she quickly added, glad Max hadn't heard her slip.

Carol smiled. "Max was a real grump about that. The stain came right out of his shirt, by the way. I have to get me some of those stain remover wipes."

"They save me on a daily basis."

"I think the boss must have felt a little guilty, 'cause he bought you a present."

"Really?"

"It's in your office." Carol smiled mysteriously, but offered up no more hints.

Jane all but sprinted down the hall to her office. When she got there, she found a shiny new laptop computer sitting in her chair.

A laptop? He'd bought her a laptop?

She turned to seek him out and get an explanation, but she didn't have to go far. He was standing right behind her.

"Is that for me?" She pointed to the ultra thin computer.

"Yeah. I've loaded it with the graphics program and set up the e-mail. Everything you need to work at home, if you have child-care issues."

"Oh, Max! This is so thoughtful. I've never had my own computer before. I mean, I know it belongs to the company, but—I can take it home with me? Are you sure?"

He laughed. "That's what I bought it for."

"I can practice with the graphics program after Kaylee goes to bed."

"Just make sure you don't stay up all night."

She felt the heat rushing to her face. How embarrassing and unprofessional that she'd shown up at her job looking a wreck, then had taken a nap on her boss's sofa. "I'll try not to."

She picked up the lightweight computer, sat in her chair, and opened it. "Does it have an instruction manual?"

"I'll get it for you. But it's pretty easy." He reached down and pushed a power button, and the machine hummed to life. "You haven't forgotten the Mattress Master ad, have you?"

"I'll get right on it." Actually, she had. If he hadn't reminded her, she'd have probably gotten engrossed in checking out her new toy, and then the Mattress Master deadline would come and go without her noticing.

But her own laptop! Scott had owned a laptop, of

course, but he literally hadn't let her touch it, claiming that if she used it, Kaylee would end up getting peanut butter on it or some such nonsense—as if Jane weren't smart enough to prevent that. She had wanted to get a home computer, but Scott had nixed the idea, claiming he saw no reason for her to have one.

Looking back, she realized now that was just one more way he had controlled and isolated her.

"I have a favor to ask," Max said, sounding uncharacteristically uncertain of himself.

"Anything."

"How do you feel about traveling for business?"

"Traveling?" She couldn't imagine where she would need to go. Unless…did he want her to sit in on client meetings? The thought thrilled her. She hoped to someday have more responsibility at her job. "I hadn't really thought about it. I hate to keep beating the same drum, but child care would be a big issue. If it's important, though, I can try to work something out."

"I appreciate that. In this case, however, you can bring Kaylee with you."

Take a child on business trip? "Maybe you better explain."

Max came into her office and closed the door, then settled into her office's only other chair, a small club chair that looked like an afterthought. With its red-and-yellow floral print, it didn't really match anything.

"Here's the deal. Ellen Lowenstein was quite taken with Kaylee. As she was leaving she mentioned all of us attending a baseball game in Houston. I thought she would forget, but she called and offered tickets to a game next week. We would leave after lunch on Tuesday, go to the game that night, stay over, and the next day we would tour the Kidz'n'Stuff offices and the manufacturing plant, stay for lunch, then drive home Wednesday afternoon."

Jane couldn't help the excitement that bubbled over. "That sounds wonderful!" It had been so long since she'd done anything so fun. A baseball game, staying at a hotel, eating at restaurants, learning how children's clothes are made. She thought Kaylee would love it, too.

Max smiled. "Great. We'll do it, then. Um, there's just one little hitch."

"I'm happy to do work while I'm there," Jane volunteered. "With the laptop I can work in the car, and at the hotel after Kaylee goes to bed—"

"That's not it, though I appreciate the offer. See…one of the reasons Ellen Lowenstein is leaning toward giving her account to the Remington Agency is because…well, because she wants Kaylee in the ads. She thinks Kaylee has the perfect look. And she wants us…you and Kaylee…to meet with a kids' modeling agency in Houston. It could mean extra money for you—lots of money, actually."

Jane was stunned. Kaylee, a model? "This is kind of a big deal," she said. "I would have to think about it. I'm not sure I want Kaylee posing in front of cameras, being the center of attention. It would take her away from her preschool and…well, I don't want to rule it out, either," she added hastily. "What a great opportunity for her to earn money for her college fund!"

"You don't have to make a decision right away. But would you be willing to meet with the agent?"

"Sure, it wouldn't hurt to just talk."

"Great. I'll make all the arrangements. Oh, Jane, there's just one more thing."

"What?"

"We have to pretend to be married."

Chapter Five

Jane's mouth opened, but no words came out.

Max probably shouldn't have sprung it on her like that, so he backpedaled. "Ellen assumed Kaylee was my daughter, since she climbed into my lap, and I didn't disabuse her of that notion."

Jane continued staring, waiting for more of an explanation.

"I think she would prefer to give her advertising account to a family man, someone who really understands what it means to be a parent. Her reaction to Kaylee was so positive, I didn't have the heart—or the courage—to tell her I'm single with no kids."

"I see. I think."

"Jane…I know it's wrong to mislead her. But I need this account. I really, really need this account, and I can do a great job on it. Maybe I'm not a parent, but I'm not completely ignorant of children. Between you and me, I know we can give this account what it needs and deserves, and everyone will be happy, and that's what's important, right?"

"I...no. I can't condone lying, Max."

"We're not really lying. Just not telling the whole truth."

Jane narrowed her eyes. "You're quibbling."

He sighed. "You're right." Now he felt like a slime-ball. Playing fast and loose with facts was such an in-grained habit in the advertising business, he hadn't really seen it as a big deal. Once he landed the account, he probably would have little or no personal contact with Ellen Lowenstein, so he would have no need to maintain the family ruse. But that didn't make it right.

"You should tell her the truth."

"I know." He thought for a minute. "Okay, how about this? We all go to the game, and I explain the situation then." *After* Ellen had a chance to see Max interact with Kaylee, see that he really was good with kids and that, if he were a father, he would be a good one.

"Well..."

"After all, my omission of the truth shouldn't get in the way of Kaylee's modeling gig. Ellen was entranced with Kaylee's picture long before she came to believe Kaylee was my daughter."

"You promise to tell Ellen the truth?"

"I will. But can we at least pretend to be...involved?"

"Max."

"Close friends? Come on, Jane. We are getting to be friends."

"You're my boss. How will Ellen feel about your being involved with your employees?"

Max thought of the proprietary glances Ellen gave Ogden from time to time. "I don't think she'd mind."

"All right. We'll go to the baseball game. How will we handle the overnight accommodations?"

Max grinned. "I'll take care of that." Remington Industries owned the Hotel Alexander, a luxury hotel in a historic downtown Houston building. Maybe he still had enough status as a Remington to get a comped suite.

"Why does that smile you're wearing give me an uneasy feeling?"

Maybe because for just an instant, Max had let himself picture himself and Jane alone in a hotel room. "Can't imagine why."

"I CAN'T BELIEVE you're going out of town with him." Allie, done with her fishing cruises for the day, had come over to kibitz while Jane packed for her overnight in Houston. "I can't *believe* you're going to pretend to be married to him. What got into you?"

"I'm not pretending anything. Okay, which of these is better for the baseball game?" She showed Allie two choices, a red halter top and a more conservative polka-dot T-shirt.

"You're asking me? I'm not exactly a fashion plate. You need Sara. She's a shopping maniac."

"Oh, right." Jane settled on the polka dots. The halter was too revealing. "I seem to recall Sara helping you pick out clothes for…what was that? A trade show in Houston? With your boss, Cooper?" Although Allie had never forked over the details of that trip, Jane knew that was how Allie and Cooper ended up in bed the first time.

Allie blushed prettily. "He was my partner, not my boss, but that's beside the point. Are you hoping you and Max will follow in our footsteps?"

"Allie, of course not!" Jane realized her denial was perhaps too fast, too emphatic. "Never mind that he's my boss. He doesn't date women with children, and I don't date, period. The ink is barely dry on my divorce decree."

Allie laughed. "Trust me when I say a whole boatload of reasons for staying apart can go right out the window in a hurry once you're alone with him—"

"Shh. Little pitchers." Kaylee was already asleep in her bunk, but she could wake up and overhear.

"But that hotel! You have no idea what a place like that does to your senses. It's like being in an amusement park. For adults."

"I have stayed in luxury hotels many times. Now, which do you like better, the pink or the purple?" She held up two sets of Kidz'n' Stuff overalls.

"The purple, I think. But what about that cute shorts outfit with the blue flowers?"

"Would you believe it's too small? Kaylee is growing so fast, she can hardly fit into any of those beautiful, expensive clothes I bought her when I still had Scott's credit card."

"Sara might like them, if she has a girl."

"I'll ask her. But that doesn't solve my current packing problem. I want Kaylee to look her best."

"Are you really going to do the modeling thing?" Allie asked, jumping in to hang up the clothes that had been discarded.

"I don't know yet. Depends on what's involved. This sounds selfish, but I'd rather keep working as an artist, even at a paltry salary, than become a stage mother to a high-fashion child model earning big bucks."

"You really love your new job?"

"I really do. I feel so alive when I'm using my creativity. I'm finally doing something that matters." At least, it mattered to Max. He was a hard taskmaster, but also generous with his praise. She lived to hear him tell her she'd done a good job. It was embarrassing, how her mood hung on his every word.

She tried not to place too much importance on that. It would be the same with any boss, she reasoned. She just wanted to succeed at a job that used her creativity. Scott had scoffed at the idea that she was even employable. He'd thought her "little art degree" was a joke. Her parents had sent her to college only because a society wife was expected to be educated, not because they expected her to do anything with the degree.

She wanted to prove all of them wrong.

"I'm so glad your job is working out," Allie said.

"Me, too. So it's doubly important I don't mess things up by making this trip to Houston something it isn't. I'm helping Max to make a good impression on his potential client. And if that means putting Kaylee in the magazine ad, I'll do that, too. But that's it. Really."

Allie sighed.

"What?"

"I just think you and Max would be cute together. Even if he does claim to not like kids."

That stopped her. "He actually doesn't like kids?"

"He's never said so. But he has a policy of not dating women with children," Allie clarified. "So I gather he's not that crazy about them."

Jane thought back to his attitude her first week at the Remington Agency. Maybe he really didn't like children. Just because he'd playacted for Ellen Lowenstein's sake didn't mean anything.

"Well, that does it, then," Jane said with finality. "I'm not going to even think about hooking up with some guy who doesn't like kids, even if he were willing, which he apparently isn't. So stop playing matchmaker. You've got romance on the brain."

"But romance is nice. A lot nicer than I imagined." She got that dreamy look in her eye, the one she got whenever her thoughts turned to Cooper.

Jane rolled her eyes. "Just because you fell in love with a Remington doesn't mean everyone has to."

"Sara did. She had worse odds than you to overcome."

"I beg to disagree. No, Allie. No, no, no. Get it out of your mind."

Allie sighed again. "We'll table this discussion. For now. But when you get back from Houston, I want a full report."

JANE COULDN'T REMEMBER the last time she'd been to a baseball game. When she was dating Scott, probably, back when he was still trying to impress her as well as his boss. Before the game Scott had critiqued every aspect of her appearance down to the height of her heels and her color of nail polish. Then they'd sat in his company's box, and Scott had paraded her in front of the company muckety-mucks like so much eye candy.

Which was exactly what she'd been. He'd even told her not to talk too much at the game, not that she'd wanted to because all anyone wanted to talk about was technology and the stock market.

Today's experience was shaping up to be quite different. For one thing, she wore flip-flops and had her hair pulled back in a ponytail.

For another, they actually watched the game. Ellen Lowenstein was a rabid Astros fan. When they did talk, it was about kids and families and hometowns. Ellen was a widow with no children, as it turned out, but she loved kids and had naturally fallen into designing children's clothes after a college internship with another kids' clothing label. She had loads of nieces and nephews, many of whom she'd invited to tonight's game, so their luxurious skybox was in a constant state of happy uproar.

Max pulled Jane into his conversation with Ellen at every opportunity. But at no time did he mention that he and Jane weren't married. Kaylee split her time playing with the other kids, eating popcorn, and crawling on whatever adult would pay attention to her. Max was one. He seemed surprisingly natural with Kaylee and the other children. More playacting? Or did he have another reason for staying away from single moms?

After Kaylee referred to Max as "Max" rather than

"Daddy" a few times, Jane was sure Ellen would say something. But instead she just laughed. "My niece Dana refuses to call *her* father 'Daddy,' too."

Jane gave Max a pointed look, but he pretended not to see.

Finally, at the seventh-inning stretch, Jane cornered Max at the cooler, when they both went for bottled water at the same time. "Are you going to tell her?" she whispered.

Max looked pained. "It's going so well."

"It's going to go very badly if she thinks you lied to her. The longer you wait, the worse it will be."

"Does she really *have* to know? You won't even see her again after tonight."

"Maxwell Remington. You promised. You *promised* me you would tell her the truth."

"Okay, okay. Just…not here, in front of all these people. Tomorrow we'll have more of a business meeting, when we take the tour. I'll tell her then."

Jane wasn't too pleased with his procrastination. But she didn't feel mean enough to just blurt out the truth to Ellen. She did want Max to get the account, and her decision wasn't completely unselfish. If Max's agency went under, she would be without a paycheck.

"All right, but don't expect me to lie. Not outright."

"I don't."

One of the other children bumped into Max's leg. Max steadied him with an indulgent smile.

Jane's heart flipped. Allie was wrong—he was a natural with kids. Every time she saw him with Kaylee, so gentle, really listening to what she had to say and talking to her as if she was as important as any adult, she wanted to cry.

Why couldn't Scott have been that kind of father? If only he had been decent to Kaylee, Jane could have overlooked all the rest. But he'd ignored her on good days and yelled at her on bad ones. When he was home at all, which was hardly ever.

If she could find a man who would be a good father to Kaylee, she would marry him, even if she didn't love him. Her remarkable little girl deserved two caring, involved parents.

She cautioned herself not to think of Max that way. If she'd ever met a confirmed bachelor, he was it. She'd seen his "little black book," so stuffed with names and phone numbers and cross-outs that it threatened to burst its seams. She'd seen the way women threw themselves at him. Even tonight, a couple of single women in the group were flirting with him.

He shot them down, of course. He wouldn't want Ellen to think he was a philanderer. But if not for that, Jane guessed he would have had himself a conquest.

When the game was over, everyone's mood was jubilant, celebrating the Astros' win. Jane pushed her morose thoughts out of her head and joined in the laughter. How often did she get a fun-filled night like this?

Ellen had insisted they take a limo back to their hotel rather than wait in a long taxi line. Now, relaxed in the cool interior, Jane felt a strange lethargy creep over her.

Oh, yes, she could get used to this again. Being poor

was a drag. Having to worry about paying the bills, having to weigh every penny she spent and forgo so many of the luxuries that had become habit—it was a lot harder than she'd thought it would be.

Her mother, ever the font of wisdom, had suggested she find herself another rich husband as quickly as she could, and Jane had turned her nose up at the advice.

But, yeah, she could get used to this.

And she could definitely get used to pretending Max was her husband. Especially when Kaylee, exhausted from all the excitement, crawled into his lap and he cuddled her just as if she really were his daughter.

Dangerous, dangerous territory.

MAX THOUGHT HE HAD NEVER seen a more angelic little girl. When she was asleep, at least. Awake, Kaylee could scream and whine and throw things with the best of them. But asleep, she was all sugar-and-spice.

Hannah had been just a little older than Kaylee when Max and her mother, Alicia, had first started dating. Back then, Max had known nothing about children. But Hannah had accepted him readily into her life, and soon the three of them had done everything as a family— pizza nights, kids' videos. Max had even helped chaperone a slumber party, a situation that had made Cooper and Reece shudder when he told them.

It was only when Alicia had started pushing for marriage that Max had taken a step back and looked long and hard at his life. He'd come to the uncomfortable realization that he didn't love Alicia.

He loved Hannah. He loved the warm, family feel of being around the little girl and her mother, a feeling that had been totally lacking in his own childhood. But at twenty-eight years old he'd not been ready for marriage. And even if he had been, he wouldn't have married a woman he wasn't in love with.

He glanced over at Jane, who was watching him.

"She's really wiped out," she whispered, nodding to Kaylee.

"Big day."

"She didn't even have a nap today, she was so excited. She'll sleep like a stone tonight."

"That's good, because tomorrow's another big day."

The limousine stopped in front of the Hotel Alexander, and Kaylee stirred and rubbed her eyes. "We home?"

"Sort of."

The driver opened the limo door, and Kaylee clambered off of Max's lap to follow her mother as she exited the vehicle. "Mommy, look!" Kaylee tugged on Jane's clothes, pointing to a giant stuffed elephant that someone was trying to fit through the revolving door, with little success.

Jane laughed. "Uh-oh. Guess that elephant had too much dinner."

Max got out and tipped the driver, then the three of them—Max, Jane and Kaylee, the pseudo-family—headed for the hotel door.

The man with the elephant had set his stuffed toy on the ground while he shuffled his other bags and packages. The temptation was too much for Kaylee and she took off toward the giant plush animal. Unfortunately, before she could get to it an uneven paving stone tripped her up. She went flying and landed with an audible thud.

Max's heart jumped into his throat as he and Jane rushed forward, reaching Kaylee just as she started wailing in pain and outright fury.

Before Max could caution the child not to move she pushed herself up. He saw the blood on her elbow and almost passed out. She also had a small scrape on her chin.

The hotel's doorman rushed over. "Do you need medical help?"

"Yes!" Max shouted. "Call for an ambulance." Dear God, Kaylee was bleeding.

But Jane was the voice of reason. "No," she said firmly, "there's no need for an ambulance." She gathered up the distraught child, taking a quick inventory. "I think we'll be all right." She produced a tissue and blotted at the blood. "Kaylee, honey, tell me where it hurts."

She pointed to the scrape on her arm.

"Ouchy. Let's go to our room and put some medicine on that."

Kaylee continued to cry, and Jane picked her up and held her close, rocking her. "Poor sweetie. I know it hurts. It'll feel better soon."

"Are you sure nothing's broken?" Max asked. "We can take her to a doctor, or the emergency room—"

"Nothing's broken. She just tripped and scraped her arm, that's all."

Max admired the calm, soothing way Jane handled the situation. By the time they'd reached the elevator, Kaylee was more whimpering than crying, and by the time they'd reached their two-bedroom suite on the ninth floor, she'd quieted down completely. However, her big, tear-filled eyes nearly did Max in.

He didn't know how parents did it, watching their children in pain. Kaylee was nowhere near his daughter, but seeing her injured and bleeding was still traumatic.

Max was ashamed of himself, at the way he had readily pretended to be a father when he hadn't earned that right. Being a father wasn't some frivolous thing. Just because he'd held Kaylee in his lap a few times…he never should have misled Ellen. And he was determined to tell her the truth first thing tomorrow.

They had checked into their hotel earlier, but they'd been running late and so they hadn't even seen the two-bedroom suite, just had their bags sent up. Max had been looking forward to Jane's reaction to the luxurious accommodations. Women always went crazy over this hotel, with its tall ceilings and plaster moldings, the lush carpeting and silk draped everywhere.

But Jane's attention was squarely on her daughter. She took her straight into the bathroom and set her down on the counter.

"Oh, shoot, my first-aid stuff is in the other bag."

"I'll get it."

"It's the small red one."

Moments later he returned with the bag. Kaylee watched solemnly as her mother produced an antiseptic towelette to clean the scrapes. She apparently carried towelettes for every occasion.

"Ow."

Jane blew on the scrape. "Sorry. But we have to clean you up so you don't get any germs." She tried to clean the cut on Kaylee's chin, but Kaylee pushed her away.

"No, Mommy. That stuff hurts. I want Max to fix me."

"Me?"

The child looked at him with adoring eyes. "You have Band-Aids?"

"Your mommy has bandages," Max countered.

"You put them on."

"She just wants attention from you because it's novel," Jane mumbled as she dug through her bag looking for something. "I always fuss over her. Now, Kaylee—"

"I want Max."

Chapter Six

Jane looked at Max, her eyes imploring. "It's late, and I'm in no mood for a tantrum. Do you mind?"

Max smiled. "Not at all." He didn't understand Kaylee wanting him, of all people, instead of her incredibly gentle and patient mother, but the little girl was entitled to a bit of spoiling after her accident. That road rash on her arm probably burned like fire.

He dabbed some antibiotic ointment on the oozing scrape. Kaylee watched him with interest, but she didn't cry or try to pull away. He did the same for the tiny cut on her chin. Finally, he put bandages on her injuries. The arm took two.

"You look like you've done this a time or two," Jane said.

He had. Hannah was a typical rough-and-tumble kid, so he knew how to apply a bandage. Now that he thought about it, Hannah had enjoyed having him fuss over her, too. Maybe it was something common to girls with absent fathers. But what did he know? He was no shrink.

What he did know was that he enjoyed taking care of Kaylee. She aroused protective feelings in him that he'd pushed aside and buried years ago. And he didn't want those feelings—not at all.

He had specifically stayed away from single moms for this very reason.

But this situation was different than the one with Hannah, he reasoned. He and Jane weren't involved. If Kaylee felt a temporary attachment for him, it would end as soon as he stopped spending time with her. And, really, he would have no reason to spend time with her after they returned to Port Clara.

"I think we're done here," Max said brightly. He needed to get out of this bathroom, away from the false intimacy.

He was not going to fall into that trap again, getting cozy with a woman because he enjoyed pretending to be a family. Not that "cozy" was even a possibility with Jane.

Jane helped Kaylee down from the counter. "Let's go find your pajamas."

Kaylee squealed with delight when she saw the big canopy bed in the bedroom she and Jane would share. "It's a princess bed!"

Max smiled as he fixed himself a drink from the minibar in the sitting room that separated the two bedrooms. He felt tremendous relief that Kaylee seemed back to her old self, that the injury hadn't been more serious. As he sipped his weak gin-and-tonic, he listened to the murmur of female voices coming from the bedroom.

Peaceful. That's how he felt. Relieved and peaceful.

That wasn't a feeling he was used to. His was a world

of highs and lows, tremendous drive and energy. Always a goal in mind. He wasn't used to just sitting, enjoying a quiet moment.

Jane emerged from her bedroom looking beautiful but frazzled. "She wants a story. And she wants you to read it." Jane settled on the loveseat across from Max. "I'm sorry, but you've suddenly become her favorite person."

"I don't mind reading her a story. Does she like *Green Eggs and Ham?* I can do that one from memory."

"Really?"

Maybe he shouldn't have revealed that. He didn't want to get into his history with Alicia and Hannah, not tonight. "It's my favorite."

"She likes it, too, Sam-I-Am."

Max abandoned his drink and strolled into the bedroom. "I am Sam. Sam-I-Am."

Kaylee giggled. "No, you're Max."

As he recited the familiar text from memory, Kaylee's eyes grew heavier and heavier, and Max's eyes strayed often to the other side of the double bed, with its luxurious sheets and silk comforter, picturing Jane reclining there, her dark hair spilled over her pillow.

What did she wear to bed? A skimpy nightgown? Boxers and a tank top? Nothing?

Max forcefully corralled his thoughts. She was his employee, a single mom *and* recently divorced. Off-limits. He had no business entertaining lurid thoughts about her.

But knowing that didn't stop him. By the time he reached the part about the fox and the box, another part of his mind had Jane undressed and writhing in his arms.

"She's asleep," Jane whispered as Max neared the end of the story. They tiptoed out of the room, and Jane quietly closed the door. "I wish I could drop off to sleep that easily."

"You don't?"

"Sometimes I lay awake worrying about the future and how I'm going to provide for Kaylee. Sure, everything's okay now. But she's young and her needs are simple. What about when she gets older? She'll want a cell phone and a computer. Prom dresses. Textbooks. College tuition."

"Ex-husbands are good for that kind of thing."

"Hah." Scott would never provide for anything that wasn't specifically spelled out in their divorce agreement, not unless he underwent a major personality transformation.

Max quickly changed the subject. "You want a drink? I noticed you stayed away from the beer and wine at the ball game."

"I wanted to keep my wits about me so I wouldn't inadvertently blurt out something to Ellen that gave away our secret. And, yes, a drink would be nice. Is there wine?"

Max headed for the minibar. "Red or white?"

"White."

She shouldn't drink anything. In fact, she should just say good-night and march back into her bedroom, brush her teeth and go to bed, even if she didn't believe she could go to sleep. She was alone in a hotel suite with her boss. She thought about all those business trips Scott took. Staff development seminars, regional meetings in Dallas…

Oh, who cared about Scott.

Max handed her a glass of Chablis, and she took a sip. It was cold and crisp. "Not bad for minibar wine."

"The Hotel Alexander strives to be a cut above. It says so on all their advertising."

"Did *you* come up with that slogan?"

"Yeah. Long time ago." He reclaimed his drink—something clear with ice—and settled across from her. Well out of arm's reach, thank goodness.

"So, Max, I'm curious. Why do you have a policy of not dating women with children?"

He scowled. "Where'd you hear that?"

"From Allie. Or Sara—I can't remember."

"You shouldn't listen to gossip."

"So it's not true?"

He didn't answer right away. In fact, he looked troubled, and Jane's heart sank. Of course they couldn't date, it was ridiculous. She had just ended one unhappy marriage and had no business even thinking about getting involved again. Yet…

Oh, Jane. She really should cut down on her fantasizing.

"I have dated women with children," he finally said. "But I found it…complicated."

"You seem good with kids, though."

"I like kids. It's not that."

"Then what? I know I'm being nosy, but I'm curious. And since I'm not auditioning for the role of your girl-friend, you can be perfectly honest."

He raised one eyebrow at her. "All right, I'll be brutally honest. Women with children are so often looking for fathers for their kids. That's what they see when they see me—a good provider as well as a guy who gets along well with children. I don't like being seen as just a potential stepfather."

"That's a bit harsh."

"It's true, though. If you were a single man out in the dating world, you would see that. Not that it's wrong for a woman to put her child first. I'm sure if you were looking for a boyfriend, your first concern would be for Kaylee. Right?"

Since her thoughts had been running along that very line earlier in the evening, she couldn't very well deny it. "Maybe you do have a point."

"It's a shame, though," he added absently, almost to himself.

"What's a shame?"

He looked up, surprised. Maybe he hadn't meant to say those words aloud. "It would be pointless to deny that I'm attracted to you, and I suspect you don't find me repulsive. Here we are in this romantic hotel, and under other circumstances…"

"Don't even think about it."

"It's hard to think about anything else."

Every cell in Jane's body came to life. Something fluttered in her stomach and her palms grew damp.

Suddenly he smiled. "Don't worry, Jane. I would never act on it. I do have some scruples."

She allowed herself to breathe again, relieved at his words. Because if he tried to seduce her, she wasn't sure she was strong enough to say no.

MAX LAY AWAKE in his big bed, still unable to sleep. The gin hadn't helped; neither had clearing the air with Jane. He wanted her just as badly as ever. Despite his brave words about having scruples, it took every ounce of his willpower not to get out of bed and knock on her bedroom door.

But he made it until morning without succumbing to temptation. When he emerged from his room, showered, shaved and dressed, he found Jane and Kaylee sitting together on the sofa. Jane was reading a book aloud in a soft voice, something a bit more complex than *Green Eggs and Ham.*

"Max!" Kaylee jumped off the sofa and ran toward him, attaching herself to his leg.

"Good morning to you, too." He ruffled her blond curls and tried not to notice how his heart squeezed painfully. How could Jane ever wonder why he avoided single moms when she saw this? He'd barely scratched the surface of his reasons last night. He hadn't mentioned that the worst thing, the very worst, was the attachment to the child—an attachment that would have to be painfully severed if things didn't work out.

It wasn't just the woman who saw him in the daddy role. With Hannah, he'd adopted it willingly.

He resisted the urge to show Kaylee more affection, though she obviously craved it. He gently detached her from his leg. "Do I smell coffee?"

"I made a pot," Jane said. "I know we're going for breakfast, but I thought we might both need some caffeine."

"You didn't sleep well, either, huh?" His voice was laced with more innuendo than he'd intended.

She arched one eyebrow at him. "I slept fine, just not long enough."

Max poured himself a half mug of coffee, wishing he had time to linger over it. Instead he gulped down a few scalding swallows. They were scheduled to meet Ellen and Ogden at the hotel restaurant in five minutes. "We probably should get going."

"I'm ready."

As they rode down in the elevator, Jane asked, "Is there some point at which you'd like me and Kaylee to disappear? I don't want Kaylee to distract from a business meeting."

"We'll see how it goes." Once he told Ellen the truth about his relationship with Jane and her daughter, Ellen might be the one who disappeared.

He was more nervous about losing this account than he cared to admit. He had payments to make on his business loan, and he shuddered to think what would happen if he was late.

Reece wouldn't be happy with him, that was for sure.

He wished he'd saved more money during the years he'd worked for Remington Industries. But back then, he'd seen money as a never-ending river. He could spend it because he would always have more.

He'd thought that by now, he would have landed some bigger accounts. But the river was more like a trickle.

"You're going to tell Ellen the truth as soon as we sit down," Jane said suddenly. "Right?"

"Yes." No matter how hard that was.

JANE COULDN'T HELP but be impressed with the beautiful hotel restaurant. She'd been to plenty of fancy restaurants before, but not with Kaylee. Scott had not believed in taking children out to eat.

In truth, sometimes a screaming toddler could be a problem at a nice restaurant. But Kaylee was almost old enough that she could be counted on to behave civilly.

She took in the high ceilings and ornate gold-leaved moldings with big eyes. "Mommy, I think a princess lives here."

"You're the only princess around," Jane replied with a slight smile.

"Your party is here," the hostess replied when Max gave his name. "Right this way."

Ellen Lowenstein and the same man who'd been with her the other day were seated at a large, round table. The man stood and extended his hand to Max.

"Remington. Good to see you again." Then he turned toward Jane. "Jane, isn't it? And Katy."

"Kaylee," Jane gently corrected.

Ogden didn't look all that pleased to be seeing the child again.

The waiter brought a booster seat for Kaylee. Max held Jane's chair for her. She looked at him. "Now, not later."

"Yes, um, well, thanks again, Ellen, for the baseball game. We had a great time."

"No sense in having that expensive box unless you share it," Ellen said cheerfully. "Ogden, you really should join us out there some time."

"I'm not much of a sports fan," Ogden said stiffly.

That figured, Jane thought, just as Kaylee started to squirm out of her chair. "Mommy, look, it's Daddy!"

"What?"

Every head at their table swiveled as Kaylee, slippery as a little frog, slid out of Jane's grasp and ran toward a man standing at the buffet with his back turned toward them.

Oh, please, let it not be.

Jane was out of her chair in a flash, running after Kaylee. It would be embarrassing to have her launch herself at some strange man shouting "Daddy!"

Then the man turned, and Jane saw that it was, in fact, Scott.

"Daddy!" Kaylee shouted again just as she reached him and attached herself to his leg, just as she'd done with Max a few minutes ago.

Scott looked down dispassionately. "Kaylee?" He was such a cold fish! Then he looked up and spotted Jane heading for him. His smile wasn't pleasant. "Well, look who we have here."

"Could you at least pretend to be happy to see your

daughter?" Jane hissed under her breath as she pulled Kaylee away from her father's leg.

"I am happy. I love my daughter."

Jane suspected that sentiment was for the benefit of the cool blonde who'd just sidled up to Scott, putting a proprietary hand on his arm.

"This is your daughter?" she asked, shooting a hostile look toward Jane.

"Daddy, we're gonna have waffles."

"What brings you to Houston?" Scott asked. "Are you already bored with dreary little Port Clara?"

"I'm at a business meeting. Really, I'm sorry to have interrupted your, er, breakfast." She wondered how Max was explaining Kaylee's outburst.

"A *business* meeting? Are you charging for it these days?"

The blonde looked surprised by the blunt attack, but Jane was livid. How dare he?

Only her reluctance to embarrass Max further kept her from grabbing a glass of orange juice from the buffet and dumping it over Scott's head.

Kaylee was still babbling, trying to get her father's attention. Jane took her hand. "We're leaving now."

But not soon enough. Scott's gaze wandered toward Jane's table, and recognition quickly registered on his face. "I don't believe it." He brushed the blonde off his arm and strode toward the table where Max, Ellen and Ogden sat.

Oh, God, no. "Scott, leave it alone!" she called after

him, scooping Kaylee up and hurrying to try to ward off the confrontation.

"So, Remington, you're not involved with my wife, huh?"

Chapter Seven

Max calmly set down his coffee cup as Ellen and Ogden looked on in horror. He stood up, appearing utterly unafraid. "I wasn't. But I am now. And she's your ex-wife, in case you'd forgotten."

Now the diners at neighboring tables were staring.

Jane was frozen with fear, and Kaylee continued to call for her daddy, who didn't seem to hear.

Scott balled up his fists, his eyes mere slits. "I could ruin you."

"I wouldn't try, if I were you. Not unless you want a few of your secrets out in the open. Or would you like for everyone to hear about Laura Ann?"

Laura Ann? Who was that?

Whoever she was, mentioning her name caused Scott's already short temper to snap. He cocked his arm back.

But Max ducked to the side. At the same time, he thrust his leg out in a lightning-fast kick that buckled Scott's legs. He toppled over, clutching his knee and cursing up a blue storm.

By then, the security guard from the hotel lobby had

been summoned. He apparently had seen who was the aggressor and who was merely defending himself, because he dragged Scott to his feet. "Sir, you'll have to come with me. Mr. Remington, are you all right?"

"Never better." He couldn't quite hide his smile of triumph.

Men.

Scott was too humiliated, or in too much pain, to argue. He limped away with the guard, not even giving Max or her or Kaylee a backward glance. The blonde, not so cool now, scurried after him.

"Well," Ogden said, pushing to his feet. "That was an interesting display. I take it you and Jane are not, in fact, husband and wife?"

Max deflated slightly. "No. We aren't even involved. I'm not married and I don't have any children. But I thought you would prefer to give your advertising account to a family man, so when you assumed Kaylee was mine, I chose not to correct you."

Ogden's scowl deepened, but Ellen merely stared, looking bewildered.

"We don't normally do business with people who lie and brawl in restaurants," Ogden said succinctly. "Ellen?"

Ellen looked like she wanted to say something, but in the end she followed Ogden out of the restaurant.

"That went well." Max practically fell back into his chair. He looked stunned, shell-shocked.

Jane said nothing. She had warned Max that when Kidz'n'Stuff found out about the deception, there would be some fallout. But not even she had visualized the truth coming out in such dramatic fashion.

"Mommy, I want to see Daddy," Kaylee said in a small voice.

"I know, sweetheart. You'll see him next weekend, and you'll get to spend two whole days with Grandpa Larry and Grandma Bonnie."

Max fiddled with his fork. "You still want breakfast? Or did this fiasco ruin your appetite like it did mine?"

"I'm not very hungry," Jane said. "But we should get something for Kaylee."

The waiter stopped at their table. "Breakfast is on us, Mr. Remington," he said. "Would you like to order from the menu, or have the breakfast buffet?"

"How about some waffles for the little one?" Max said.

"Of course. Would she like some juice? We have orange, grapefruit and cranberry."

"How about it, Kaylee?" Max asked. "You want juice?" He reached out to brush a strand of hair from her face, but she shrieked and hid her face against Jane's shoulder.

"You hurt my daddy!"

Kaylee's accusation was like a knife to Max's heart. Of course she would see Max as the villain. She wasn't old enough to understand the complexities of the fight she'd just witnessed. But she'd seen the outcome.

No matter what anyone else thought of Scott, he was Kaylee's father.

"Kaylee, listen to me," Jane said. "Your daddy lost his temper and tried to hit Max first. Max was only trying not to get hurt himself."

"You don't have to stick up for me," Max said, though he was honored that Jane would do so. "I shouldn't have hit back."

"You did exactly the right thing," Jane insisted. "If you hadn't taken him down, he'd have come at you again. His temper is completely out of control. For months I told him he needed counseling, but he wouldn't listen."

"I can't exactly blame him for being angry," Max said. "He thinks I stole you. If you were my wife, and I thought some guy had poached, I might get violent, too."

Jane blushed, and Max realized he might have been just a bit too passionate in stating his opinion. His feelings for Jane had gone beyond simple lust.

He decided a change of subject was in order. "You know, I think I will have some breakfast. It's free, after all. Who knows when we'll be able to set foot in a place like this again?" He certainly wouldn't be paying for fancy restaurants until the agency brought in some larger accounts. He was grateful for the Mattress Masters of the world, but he needed more.

"Are the finances in bad shape?" Jane asked.

"Not as bad as all that. But don't expect an extravagant raise any time soon."

THE PLANNED TOUR of the Kidz'n'Stuff offices and manufacturing facility was obviously off the schedule, but they still had the appointment with the modeling agency.

"Maybe we should cancel that, too," Jane said, "and

just go home." They stood in front of the hotel, waiting for the valet to bring their car around. "Clearly Ellen isn't going to want Kaylee in her ads now."

"I still think you should talk to the agent. Modeling can be incredibly lucrative."

"Have you been a model?" Jane eyed him up and down, thinking his face and body could sell jeans or motorcycles by the gazillion.

He grinned. "No, but I've hired plenty of them. In New York, some of them make hundreds of dollars an hour."

"Well, sure, the supermodels—"

"No, I'm talking about ordinary no-name models."

"Really?"

"A lot of people would kill to get an interview with this agency—it's well-known."

"All right. I guess I should keep the appointment. Though I can't imagine Kaylee's going to make a grand impression with her bandages and her attitude."

"My what?" Kaylee was always paying attention, alert for the sound of her name.

"Your mood. You're not in a very good mood this morning."

"Yes I am."

"In that case, before we visit the modeling agency, you'll let me brush your hair and put a ribbon in it."

She had to think about that one, finally agreeing with a reluctant, "Okay." Combing the tangles out of her long hair was a constant battle, but whenever Jane suggested getting it cut Kaylee threw a fit.

By the time the three of them entered the elegant office building that housed the Freeman Agency, Kaylee had, in fact, perked up. She looked adorable, with her Kidz'n'Stuff pink overalls, pink ruffled socks and miniature athletic shoes, and a pink ribbon in her hair. She even carried a tiny purple purse, which had been her idea, not Jane's. Perhaps she understood what was going on here more fully than Jane gave her credit for.

The receptionist greeted them with a haughty, down-her-nose look. She was tall and elegant, with black hair swept back into a twist. She easily could have been a model herself.

"Good morning," Jane said with confidence she didn't feel. "Jane Selwyn and Kaylee Simone, here to see Erin Freeman."

The woman consulted her appointment book. "If you'll have a seat—"

"Is this Kaylee?" A woman with flaming red hair that went in all directions and a pair of thick, blue-framed glasses had burst into the room. Jane's first thought was that she belonged on a kids' TV show.

Jane extended her hand. "This is Kaylee and I'm her mother, Jane."

"I'm Erin, pleased to meet you." Her eyes never left Kaylee. "Come on back."

"I'll wait here," Max said.

"No, please, come with us," Jane said, trying not to sound too desperate. But Max knew so much more about this stuff than she did.

Max shrugged, and they all followed Erin to her enormous corner office, which featured leather furniture and an array of kids' toys.

Erin focused her attention first on Kaylee, engaging her in conversation. Kaylee was at her friendly, cheerful best, apparently having overcome the trauma of breakfast. After a few minutes, Erin invited Kaylee to play with whatever toys she wanted, and the adult conversation started.

"Let's take a look at her portfolio."

"Um, right. She doesn't have one."

"No?"

"She's never done any modeling."

Erin looked confused. "Oh, but…what's this?" She had a color printout of the Kidz'n'Stuff comp Jane had drawn.

Jane looked at Max.

"I scanned it into the computer and e-mailed it to Ellen," Max explained.

"That's just a mock-up I did for the ad agency where I work," Jane said with a laugh. "I used a snapshot of Kaylee because I happened to have one on hand."

Erin studied the ad for almost a minute without talking. Then she looked up, her eyes alight with inspiration. "Are you represented?"

"Me? I'm not a model."

"As an artist. Although I could probably get you some print work, but if you'll forgive me, pretty women are a dime a dozen. Artists with your talent, on the other hand, are rare. Do you have an agent?"

"Well…no."

"I could get you commissions. Portrait work. I might even be able to get you into a gallery. What else do you have?"

"Um…"

"She can have her portfolio to you in a couple of weeks," Max said.

"Great."

"But what about Kaylee?" Jane squeaked.

"She needs pictures." Erin pulled a business card out of her desk drawer and handed it to Jane. "Take her to this photographer and have her headshot done. If I have that, I can get her some work. She definitely has that certain something advertisers go wild for."

Erin then pulled two more cards out, one for Jane and one for Max. "Mr. Remington, I hope you'll think of the Freeman Agency for your modeling, photography and artistic needs. We have some amazing talent in our stable. Though obviously you've got some of your own right in your backyard. I don't suppose you've done any modeling…"

"No," Max said, closing that door in a hurry.

Jane's head was spinning. Photos for Kaylee, an art portfolio for her…

She said nothing until they were in the elevator heading for the parking garage. "Why did you say that? An art portfolio in two weeks, are you insane?"

Max grinned. "I told you you were good. If Erin Freeman thinks you are, too…that's not something to sneeze at."

"But I have a job and a child to take care of. I don't have time to put together a portfolio."

"You did…what, four drawings in one night? Do a few more, and you have a portfolio. I'll give you the time off if you need it."

"But…why?" Didn't he need her? Oh, Lord, was her job in jeopardy? She always came back to that fear.

"Because you deserve to succeed. Yes, I want to keep you as an employee, but I don't want to hold you back. If something better comes along, take it. Don't worry about me."

That was just about the most unselfish thing anyone had ever said to her. No one had ever told her she deserved anything.

"Thank you, Max. But I like working at the Remington Agency. It's exciting. I might like to do portraits as a sideline… Oh, I feel so guilty."

"Guilty?"

"This was supposed to be Kaylee's chance to shine, and I stole her big moment."

"You didn't steal anything. It was handed to you. Anyway, the door is still open for Kaylee."

"Yeah, if I can come up with the money for pictures. Which really is out of the question right now. I bet this photographer charges a fortune."

"I'll pay for it."

"What? Max, no."

"She deserves—"

"I won't be in debt to you. One promise I made to myself after the divorce was that I would live within my means, no matter what. Kaylee can wait until I've saved the funds to pay a photographer."

"No strings attached."

Oh, but there would be strings. She could already feel them pulling on her, drawing her into a closer emotional bond with Max. And that was crazy—for all the reasons she'd gone over and over in her head.

"I appreciate the offer, but no," she said firmly.

The drive home was quiet. Kaylee napped through most of it, and Jane looked out the window, unable to stop herself from reliving this morning's breakfast debacle.

Then she remembered something, and she simply had to speak. "Max, who is Laura Ann, and why was mentioning her name such a threat to Scott?"

Max looked decidedly uncomfortable. "I'm not sure you want to know."

"Yeah, I do." She glanced into the backseat. "Kaylee's fast asleep. You can tell me."

Max stared straight ahead. "I didn't take it seriously when Scott said he would ruin me, but when I mentioned it to Cooper, he went into lawyer mode. He did some digging around and came up with a few skeletons in your ex's closet. Laura Ann is an old flame…"

"Go on."

"He saw her on and off through your whole marriage."

"Huh." Jane couldn't muster much of a reaction. Perhaps she'd already known, on some level, that Scott hadn't been faithful.

"I'm sorry."

She reached across and touched his arm. "No, you did the right thing, and it really doesn't bother me. I am well and truly over him."

Max smiled. "Good."

THE FOLLOWING MONDAY, as Max readied the conference room for a client meeting, he still wondered why he'd offered to pay for Kaylee's modeling photos.

Jane and Kaylee were in no way his responsibility, and it wasn't like him to just hand out money because he had a generous heart. Yeah, he used to be the guy who always bought another round of drinks and took clients and girlfriends to the most expensive restaurant in town. But he'd always had an angle.

What possible angle did he have with Jane?

It was a good thing she'd turned down his offer. He didn't have wads of disposable cash like he used to. He couldn't just go throwing it around. He needed his liquid assets to keep the agency afloat. Pay salaries. Buy food.

"Mr. Remington, your two o'clock meeting is here," Carol said over the intercom in her most obsequious voice. He had to hand it to her, she knew how to play it just right. The client was a local bank. It wasn't an account on the level of Kidz'n'Stuff, but it was decent. And the marketing guy was a stuffed shirt who would appreciate formality.

Max had actually put on a tie for the occasion.

He went to the reception area and greeted the two men and a woman who'd come for the meeting. Both men tried to crush his hand when they shook, and he struggled not to wince.

He couldn't show weakness.

When they were all assembled in the conference room, he suddenly realized he'd made a tactical error. It was three against one. He was a lone guy, which made him look like small potatoes. He needed a team, like they had.

"Excuse me for just one moment. Let me get my...associate."

He stepped into Jane's office, where she sat engrossed in her computer graphics, as usual. Even if he didn't have work for her to do, she was always experimenting with the program, learning new tricks, poring over the pages of the instruction manual with a highlighter and sticky notes.

"Jane."

She jumped, as she usually did when he interrupted her work. "What?" She blinked at him owlishly.

"I want you to sit in on my meeting with Coastal Bank."

"Really?" She stood and looked down at herself. "Do I look okay?"

More than okay. Her tailored slacks skimmed her slim hips and accentuated long legs and a tiny waist, and though there was nothing overtly sexy about her silk blouse, he could see the shape of her breasts clearly.

His mouth watered. "You look great. But grab your jacket."

"Do I have to say anything?"

"Just nod when I speak and look utterly supportive."

She smiled. "I can do that."

Max didn't waste time on idle getting-to-know-you chit-chat. He sensed this group would want to get right to it. So after a few preliminary comments, he dimmed the lights and started his PowerPoint presentation.

Max had pitched this bank because he thought their ads were stale and old-fashioned. He believed their image needed a face-lift, especially when two national banks with big budgets had opened branch offices in Port Clara in the past year.

He showed them some ideas for new logos, expertly drafted by Jane, and then some ad concepts featuring young, hip-looking people.

"But those people don't look like our customers," the marketing manager complained.

"Ah, but they *could* be your customers."

"Older people are the ones with money," the woman pointed out.

"True, but in a few years, younger people will be older, and they'll have money, too. When they start thinking about retirement funds, or college funds for the kids, wouldn't it be nice if they were already loyal to Coastal Bank?"

"But that logo," the older man complained. "It's just too modern. I wouldn't trust a bank with a logo that would be more at home on the front of a video store."

"We're certainly not married to that idea," Max said smoothly.

Jane cleared her throat. "So what you're l ooking for is a logo that says, 'We're safe, we're secure, we've been around a long time,' but also something that says, 'We're progressive, we're not stodgy or old-fashioned.'"

Max shot her a warning look, but she studiously avoided looking at him.

"Well, yes, young lady, that's exactly right."

"What if we took your current logo and modified it slightly. Keep the type, keep the colors, but clean up that ship and make it more abstract. Give everything a 3-D look."

"I'm not sure what you mean," the older man said uncertainly.

Jane whipped out her sketchpad, which she brought with her everywhere. Had she foreseen that the client wouldn't like Max's concept?

She flipped to a page that already had the beginnings of her concept. When she and Max had discussed this, he had nixed the idea. She added a few lines to the drawing. He couldn't believe how quickly the logo took shape. Rough still, but easy to visualize the end result.

The bank's team studied it. They studied it a long time.

Finally the older man looked up. "I like this. You fix this up and put it in the new ads, and I think we can do business. But…that kid with the beard. I don't want him in my ad."

"That's no problem," Max said. "You can approve the models before we move forward."

There were handshakes all around. Max agreed to meet with the team again in a week, and he and Jane walked them to the door.

Once the door to the hallway was closed, Max took

a deep breath. He waited until he was sure the bank people were safely on the elevator. Then he turned to a beaming Jane.

"What the hell did you think you were doing back there?"

Chapter Eight

Jane's stomach plummeted. Here she'd been feeling on top of the world, so pleased by the successful outcome of the meeting.

But one sharp word from Max, and she was crushed.

She straightened her spine. "I was saving your bacon, what do you think I was doing?"

"Your instructions were to smile and nod."

"I smiled and nodded for six years when I was married to Scott. I've decided I won't do that anymore. Are you saying you wish I hadn't said anything? Because those three people were getting ready to bail. You'd lost them."

"I hadn't lost them. Listen, I can persuade anyone to do anything. It's my gift."

"So you think the right thing to do was persuade them to go with a logo they didn't like?"

"That bank needs to step into the twenty-first century."

"Are you saying my ad doesn't do that? It's bold, it's modern—"

"And I told you yesterday it wouldn't work."

"But they like it," she argued.

"My job isn't just to land accounts. My job is to create advertising that pulls in business."

Carol looked on from her desk, obviously fascinated.

Jane pushed up her sleeves. "My logo is going to drive people away? Is that what you're saying?"

"You might know a lot about art, but you know nothing about marketing."

"So educate me. What, in your expert opinion, is wrong with my logo?"

"Well, it's…it's too much like their old logo."

Jane took a step back. She walked to the coffeemaker and poured herself some in a foam cup, giving herself time to think. He was her boss, and she was obligated to do what he said. But he was also being pigheaded here.

"I think you don't like it because you didn't think of it. You want to be the boy genius behind everything. It's why you didn't show Kidz'n'Stuff the sketch I did with my own concept. You want to keep me in my place."

"Whoa, girl," Carol said, a cautionary note in her voice.

Max stomped around the reception room. There wasn't much room to stomp, so he ended up right next to her again. The frond from an overhead Boston fern tickled his hair, and he brushed it away, annoyed. "That is so utterly not true. I believe in teamwork."

"Then why did you tell me I should just smile and nod during the meeting?"

Carol's jaw dropped. "Max, you didn't really say that, did you?"

"Because each person on the team," Max said steadily, "needs to work to their own strengths."

"Fine. I'll stick to my colored pencils and I won't say a word. But don't ask me to any more meetings. Do you want me to work up that logo or not?"

"We're committed to it now."

"I guess that's a yes."

"Work it into the ads. I'll see if I can find some stock photos of young people without beards. I'll need it all by the meeting next week."

"Yes, sir." She clicked her heels and stalked out of the room. Okay, maybe she'd gone too far. He was the boss. He signed her paychecks. But she couldn't sit by and let that account slip out the door.

She wanted a career that allowed her to use her brain as well as her creativity. She'd thought Max valued her opinions. But apparently she'd been wrong.

Maybe she would get to work on that portfolio for the agent. She would need the portrait thing to fall back on when Max fired her.

"THAT WASN'T PRETTY," Carol said, clearly amused.

"Don't start on me. You didn't see it—she took over the whole damn meeting."

"And that wounds your male ego."

"It's not that. It's just…"

"You landed the account. Aren't you happy about that?"

"Sure, but now I have to deliver results. I'm not sure I can."

"Because…why, exactly?"

He didn't know. Jane's logo was fine. More than fine, it was good. She had sensed exactly what the client wanted, and she'd delivered it in a way that should have made everyone happy.

So why wasn't he happy? Was it simply because they'd liked Jane's idea better than his? Was he that shallow?

"I'm going to lunch."

"Okay."

"Maybe while I'm gone you could…unruffle some feathers?"

"I can try, but she was pretty steamed."

"Just don't let her quit, okay? I need her."

And he wanted her, worse than ever.

He thought about heading to Old Salt's for a burger. But instead he called Reece. "Want me to bring over some takeout?"

"Be still my heart. Sara has me eating so much salad and baked chicken it's coming out my ears. I'd kill for a greasy burger and fries."

"I'll get us chicken sandwiches." He wasn't going to risk Sara's wrath. Reece had been on the fast track to a heart attack before Sara had gotten hold of him, and Max wasn't going to be an enabler. He could probably stand to improve his diet, too, since it was *his* father who'd had the heart attack a few years ago.

"To what do I owe the honor of your presence?" Reece asked a few minutes later. They were sitting at the B and B's kitchen table, digging into their sandwiches. "You've been so wrapped up with work, we've hardly seen you."

"I'm trying to turn a profit. It's not going too well."

"Sounds like something I should know about."

He couldn't meet Reece's steady gaze. "I lost the Kidz'n'Stuff account."

"Damn."

"But that's not what I came to talk about. I have a bigger problem than cash flow."

Reece looked confused. "Is there a bigger problem than cash flow?"

"Jane."

"Ahhhhhh. We all saw that one coming, dude. All of us but you, anyway. Did you cross the line?"

"No. I haven't touched her. But it's killing me. Seeing her every day, smelling her perfume or shampoo or whatever it is. And even if she didn't work for me…there's Kaylee."

Reece nodded. He, if anyone, would understand. He'd been around during the Max and Alicia breakup fiasco. "You don't want another Hannah situation on your hands."

"Exactly. During the trip to Houston, when I was pretending that Jane and Kaylee were my family…it felt good. Incredibly good."

"Really?"

Of course Reece would be surprised. Max hadn't acted like a man ready to settle down, especially over the past few years. After Alicia he had played the field like a madman, never dating the same woman more than a month or two.

"I could never see myself married to Alicia. But Jane is different."

"So you might bend your 'no dating single moms' rule for her?"

He thought about Kaylee, about how she'd pushed him away after she'd seen him bring her father down. It still stung. How much worse would it be if they truly bonded and then things ended badly? "I don't want to hurt Kaylee."

"It's not like you to be fearful of risk. Cooper and I have spent half our lives pulling you back from the brink of one disaster or another because you *are* fearless."

Max pondered that as he sucked down the last of his root beer. He'd risked all of his personal wealth on a business venture. But one little blond girl and her mother scared him to pieces.

"Even if I wanted to go for it," he finally said, "I can't. She's my employee. And don't tell me to fire her."

"Find her another job, then."

"I can't. I need her."

"You could find another artist. Didn't you have three or four panting for the job a couple of weeks ago?"

"Jane is more than an artist. She's brilliant with the clients. She comes up with concepts. I landed Coastal Bank today because of her."

"You've answered your own question, then. You can't date her."

"I know that." Maybe he'd just wanted someone else, someone he trusted, to confirm it.

"Or maybe you're just using the boss-employee thing as an excuse because you're afraid."

Max didn't dignify that observation with a response.

Reece polished off his sandwich and wiped his mouth. "Thanks for lunch."

"Thanks for being a sounding board. I think."

"Any time. What else can I do for you?"

"Can you get me an extension on my business loan?"

"I told you you spent too much on the remodeling."

"I don't need a lecture, I need cash. Payroll is coming up. I've hired two new account executives and a media buyer."

"I'll try to get the extension. But you can always borrow a little from me or Coop."

Max shook his head. "No. I have to do this on my own. After the way I left Remington Industries, burning all my bridges because I was so confident, I can't go borrowing from family, not even you guys. Especially you guys. You're newlyweds, you and Sara have a kid on the way, you're both trying to run businesses of your own."

Reece nodded. "Okay. But we're here if you change your mind. Whatever you do, do *not* default on that loan. You know who holds it, right?"

"Uh, no." He never paid attention to that stuff, he just signed papers and spent the money.

"Coastal Bank."

"HE DIDN'T MEAN IT," Carol said. "It's just that male ego thing."

Jane studied her computer screen, refusing to even look up. "That's no excuse. His attack was completely unjustified. When I first took this job, you said he was fair."

"He is…most of the time. You're not going to quit, are you?"

"And do what? I have mouths to feed. Is that all Max is worried about? Making sure I don't quit?"

Carol came all the way into Jane's office and settled in the ugly flowered chair. "You know why this is happening, don't you?"

"Yeah, because Max is a jerk."

"The tension between you two has been building since the day you arrived. I can feel it in the air every time you're in the same room. Something had to give. Either you were going to have a big fight or you were going to wind up in bed."

That made Jane look up. Was she really that transparent? "You're crazy."

"No, I'm not," Carol said with utter certainty. "Personally, if it was me, I'd stop fighting and go with plan B. The constant tension is going to make it hard for you to work together."

"We can't," Jane almost wailed, realizing too late she'd just admitted to Carol that she was right. "He's my boss, and it's unethical."

"Oh, please. People who work together do it all the time. If we worked in a big corporation where there was a policy against it, that would be one thing. But we're just a little company."

Jane shook her head. "Workplace romances are a bad idea. Sure, it's fine at first, but what about when things don't work out? Then people quit or get fired, which can lead to jealousies, charges of harassment…"

She had no firsthand experience about this, but she'd heard stories of what went on at Scott's office.

Carol rolled her eyes. "Can you see anyone around here who would sue anybody else? And who would be jealous? Not me. I don't need a man in my life."

"Exactly! Neither do I. What I do need is this job. I love this job, even if my boss does behave like a jerk. I'm not going to mess things up because of a few hormones."

"Well, I think you're crazy, throwing away a fine man like Max Remington. How many women would give up their hair extensions to hook up with him?"

Jane saved her file and turned away from her computer. It wasn't as if she was actually getting any work done. "Plenty do go out with him. Have you ever seen his little black book? He left it open on his desk once, and I couldn't help but see it. He actually puts stars by their names."

"Was your name in there?"

"I don't know." He'd walked in before she could flip to the S's.

A soft knock sounded on the door, and Jane's heart did a little dance. She wasn't ready to face him yet. She didn't have her temper completely under control, and she didn't trust herself to behave rationally.

"Come in," Carol sang out, as if she had the perfect right to. "I was just leaving." She scurried out behind Max, giving Jane a mischievous wink over her shoulder just before disappearing.

The look on Max's face nearly did her in. He was actually nervous about facing her.

"If you're here to lecture me," she began, going on the offensive, but he cut her off.

"No more lectures." That was when he produced the flowers, which he'd been holding behind the door. Roses. Red roses. A dozen of them.

No one had brought her flowers since…well, since the last time Scott had tried to win her back after she filed for divorce. She'd thrown them in the trash.

They're just flowers. But she knew these wouldn't end up in any Dumpster.

"I was totally out of line," he said, laying the flowers on her desk. The heady scent of roses filled her nose and softened her brain. "You were right. It was my ego. From the start, this agency has been my baby. At my old job, I never got credit for my ideas 'cause I was just part of a big team. This time around, I didn't want to share credit for any success.

"But that's just stupid. A company is only as good as the people working there. You're my greatest asset, a talented artist with marketing instinct and people skills. Thank you for saving the Coastal Bank account."

"I…um, you're welcome." Jane couldn't seem to come up with anything more intelligent to say. She hadn't been expecting an apology, much less for Max to admit he'd been wrong. Scott's apologies had always been something like, "I'm sorry you're upset," as if he'd had nothing to do with it.

"I would give you a raise," Max said, "but I can't."

"I don't need a raise," she lied. They stared at each other for several long seconds. Finally Jane couldn't stand the silence—she had to fill it. "The roses need water. I don't have a vase."

She pushed up from her desk and walked around it, dangerously close to Max.

He picked up the flowers again and extended them to her. "I didn't know what kind of flowers you like, but the florist said roses were pretty safe."

She paused and smiled. "No sane woman dislikes roses." She took the flowers, immediately surrounded again by their heady scent. She closed her eyes so she could isolate the sensation and experience it fully.

"Jane?"

Her eyes flew open and she smiled. "Sorry, I was on a little mental vacation. Where can I find a vase?"

"You're asking a guy, remember. Try the kitchen, maybe."

Jane hurried out of her office before she did something crazy, like touch Max. Like hug him for taking the time and care to make this gesture, to make her feel valued.

Yes, that was what Max did that no one else ever had. He made her feel valued not for her looks, but her abilities.

Max followed her into the break room, and they both started opening cabinet doors, searching for a proper container for the flowers. Unfortunately, they came up empty.

"I have an idea." Max exited the kitchen, and Jane followed, curious. He went to one of the unoccupied offices, which were still unfinished. "Just as I thought." The workmen had left an empty bucket, which had once been filled with paint.

"Why, what a lovely vase."

"Hey, do you want your roses to wither?"

"I suppose I shouldn't complain. You did buy the flowers, after all."

They rinsed out the bucket and filled it at the sink in the break room. Then Max set it on a table, and Jane unwrapped the flowers and put them in the water, rear-ranging them until she was satisfied.

She admired the effect. "Hmm. Kind of kitschy. Maybe we've started a new decorating trend. I can see fashionable matrons all over the country putting spat-tered paint buckets filled with roses in their living rooms."

She looked up to see if her lame joke had scored with Max, but he wasn't smiling. He was looking at her with such naked longing on his face that her knees turned soft and she went light-headed.

"Your smile is so pretty." His voice was ragged. "Not even a dozen roses outshine you."

The compliment was so simple and heartfelt that it brought tears to Jane's eyes. "Th-thank you."

"I want to touch you. But you're so perfect I'm afraid to."

"Max…you really better stop there." Although she didn't want him to. She wanted him to push those flowers out of the way and come across the table at her. She wanted him to push her against the wall and kiss her until she ran out of breath. She wanted to feel his body pressed up against hers, all that hard mascu-linity…

"I can't think about anything else. Are you saying you don't feel the same way?"

She felt exactly the same way. She didn't go five minutes without thinking about him. Even when she was angry with him, sensual images of him, of them together, plagued her.

Could she lie? Could she look him in the eye and say she didn't want him? If she could, it would make all of their lives simpler. She did not need another man in her life, and neither did Kaylee, not unless that man would stick around forever.

Yes, closing the door firmly on any type of personal relationship was the sane, wise thing for her to do. Max would totally respect her decision. She knew that about him.

She looked him in the eye, steadily, and stiffened her spine, rehearsing exactly what she would say. She opened her mouth, intending to be firm but kind. But what she said was, "I want you worse than I've ever wanted anyone in my whole life."

Chapter Nine

Max knew what he did in the next five seconds would have a profound impact on his life. He might cause Jane to quit. He might open himself up for a sexual harassment lawsuit. Or he might be involving himself with a woman on the rebound from a bad marriage—never a good idea.

At the moment, though, he didn't care about any of that stuff. He just wanted Jane in his arms. And she wanted the same thing.

Her reaction surprised him. He'd been counting on her to be the voice of sanity. But sanity was noticeably absent from the room.

Just one kiss. That was all he wanted. That was what he told himself, anyway.

The air between them crackled with electricity and time slowed to a crawl. Max deliberately stepped around the table, and in two strides he was there. He grasped her delicate shoulders and backed her up against the wall. She stared up at him with huge eyes, her moist lips parted slightly, her breasts rising and falling rapidly.

"Last chance to say no."

She remained silent, so he leaned in and captured those enticing, full lips with his—and was immediately in a different world. The room around them fell away. Time and space were nonexistent. There was only Jane, the feel of her, the scent of her, the wanting that welled up in her as palpable to him as his own desire.

Her response was quick and intense. She kissed him like she wanted to inhale him, snaking her arms around his neck, her fingers grabbing handfuls of his hair—

"Hello, where is everybody?"

Max and Jane sprang apart, instantly putting six feet between them, but it was too little too late. Carol was halfway into the break room already.

She skidded to a stop. "Oh. Ohh."

Max wanted to object to her reaction, to stop the thoughts running through Carol's head, but what could he say? Denials were useless.

"What is it, Carol?"

"Those real-estate magazines are here. Where do you want them?"

"In, um, in the storeroom." His brain was having a hard time coming back to life.

"Okay."

Carol backed out of the room with a wink.

"Oops." Jane sank into the nearest chair. "That was less than discreet of us."

Max had no idea what to say. He'd never jumped an employee before. "I, um, better check on those magazines."

"I didn't know we were printing any real-estate magazines."

"It was a job we did before I hired you. In fact, working with the freelancer in Dallas was such a bad experience, it convinced me to hire someone on staff."

Max felt some measure of relief that he was still capable of a normal conversation—and that Jane didn't seem to be mad at him, though what he'd done was inexcusable. Yes, she'd been a willing participant, but he'd started it. He'd taken advantage of her.

"Let's go have a look at the magazines."

"Um, Max…" She gestured for him to wipe his mouth. "You have my lipstick all over your face."

He smiled at her. "You have it all over yours, too."

As soon as they'd repaired the damage with another of Jane's ever-handy wipes they went to the storeroom, where a deliveryman with a dolly stacked up five boxes.

"How many boxes are there?" Max asked.

"That's all," the man said with a shrug.

"What? That can't be right. You can't fit ten thousand magazines into five boxes."

The man shrugged. "That's all I have."

Maybe the rest were coming later, Max reasoned. They still had a few days before their deadline. But he got an uneasy feeling in his gut.

"Ten thousand?" Jane said. "That's a lot of magazines."

"It's my biggest job so far. Not that I'm making a whole lot of profit. I bid the job low because I really wanted the account. But if the client is pleased, we might be doing this monthly, so there's potential for the future."

He grabbed a box cutter and sliced open one of the cartons. When he saw what was inside, he nearly passed out.

The magazines were pink. Everything had an unhealthy pink tinge—the photos, the background, the type.

Jane gasped. "Are they supposed to look like that?"

"Hell, no!"

"Maybe it's just the one carton."

Max sliced open another carton, and then a third, but they all looked the same. Pink.

"Good gravy," Carol said under her breath.

This was bad. This was worse than bad, this was an unmitigated disaster.

"We don't have to pay for these, do we?" Carol asked.

"We've already paid half up front." He strode to his office, intending to get the artist on the phone and find out what had happened. These magazines didn't look anything like the proof he had approved. Obviously the artist hadn't gone to the printers to approve the printed proof, as he'd said he would.

The artist's phone rang and rang. No answer.

"Damn it!"

Jane stood at the door. "What can I do?"

"I don't know. The client is expecting ten thousand four-color magazines in five days. Five hundred pink magazines isn't going to make a favorable impression."

"You can't call the printer and insist they do these over? And print the correct number?"

The printer. Of course. What kind of idiots printed five hundred pink magazines and thought that was just fine?

Max had never worked with this particular printer; they were some outfit the artist had claimed was great.

Perfect Printing. Max checked the return address label. It was a P.O. box. He looked them up on the Internet and couldn't find them. He called Dallas information. No phone listing.

What was going on here?

The situation disintegrated from there. By the end of the day, Max was forced to conclude that he'd been bamboozled. The artist had screwed up the job so badly that he'd gone into hiding. The printer was probably some friend or relative with a printing press in his garage who had no clue what he was doing. When they'd realized the job was far beyond their capabilities, they'd split the money and run.

Max felt sick. Not only had he wasted money he couldn't afford to lose, his reputation would be in shreds once the client learned what had happened.

Was this it, then? Would he have to close the agency in disgrace and crawl home, begging for his old job back? He could just imagine what his older brother, Eddie, would have to say about that.

Jane felt terrible about what was happening. She'd tried to be as supportive as possible, calling people and chasing down information when she could, or sitting in her office working on the computer when she could do nothing else.

Now, at the end of the day, the news wasn't good. It seemed Max had no way out of this dilemma.

"Do you have the original art?" Jane asked. She stood at Max's office door, wanting to do something, *anything,* to take that look of utter defeat off Max's face.

"I have the page proofs on my computer...somewhere."

"We could find another printer."

"Finding a printer who can do a job this size in under five days...it's impossible. Even if we found someone, the expedite fees would be staggering."

"Wouldn't losing some money on the job be better than losing the client?"

"Sure. But the brutal truth is, I don't have the money."

"How much do you think it would take?"

He threw out a figure that made Jane nauseous. It rivaled her annual salary.

"Maybe we could get the money somehow. Or get a loan."

"I've already reached my credit limit."

Jane refused to be defeated. "You find the printer. I'll try to find the money."

"Jane, I appreciate your enthusiasm, but where would you find the money? Last I heard, you didn't have enough to fill your gas tank."

True enough. But that was *her* money. She knew lots of rich people. "Let me try."

"I would need an answer quickly. Any printer who agreed to the job would give me a narrow window, and I would have to commit. I'm not going to commit when I know I can't pay."

"I understand." She looked at her watch. It was after five. She would be late picking up Kaylee, but Mrs. Billingsly, the woman who ran the after-school program, was far more lenient than the school about tardiness, so she wasn't too worried. "I'll have an answer by tomorrow morning."

Finally he smiled. "Thanks, Jane. You don't have to take this on as your problem, you know. I don't pay you enough for that."

"But it is my problem. If your agency goes under, I'm out of a job."

"The agency won't go under." But he didn't sound completely convinced of that himself. "Listen, Jane, about what happened…" He nodded in the general direction of the kitchen, and she nodded back. "I was out of line. Way out. There's no excuse for it."

Jane swallowed, her mouth suddenly dry as old parchment. She'd been trying, mostly unsuccessfully, to put it out of her mind, to write it off as one insane moment to be forever cherished but never repeated.

"It's okay," she said.

"It won't happen again."

Was she supposed to be relieved? Because all she felt was supreme disappointment. "Are you sure about that?"

"No."

She applauded his honesty, at least. Her heart lifted. She felt clueless in this situation, but apparently so did he. "I'll see you tomorrow." She made a quick escape before she said or did anything foolish. More foolish.

Tonight, she would think hard about what to do with

Maxwell Remington. After she swallowed her pride and called her parents to beg for a loan.

"MOMMY, WHO'S THAT MAN?" Kaylee asked as she and Jane made their way from the parking lot to the dock.

Jane tensed. There was, in fact, a man loitering on the dock near the *Princess II*. After a few moments, he heaved a wistful sigh and moved on, stopping to look at another pretty cabin cruiser.

"I think he's just admiring the boats," Jane said, relaxing. The man's interest wasn't unusual; her boat had always attracted attention. It had certainly attracted hers six years ago when she and Scott had bought it. They'd gotten unsolicited offers on it several times—

Wait a minute. The answer to her dilemma was right under her nose.

Jane picked up the pace. As soon as she was inside her boat, she dropped everything and headed straight to the fold-down desk next to the galley where she kept all her papers.

"What are you doing?" Kaylee asked.

"Mommy's had a brainstorm." She rummaged around until she found the business card she was looking for. Dave Shenkler. He was the CEO of some Internet auction site, and he was rolling in money. A couple of weeks ago, Jane had discovered him and his wife standing on the dock, admiring the *Princess II*. He had offered to buy it on the spot, and Jane had automatically turned him down.

But the *Princess II* was worth a lot of money— enough to bail out the Remington Agency and then some.

Everyone had told her she ought to sell it and use the money to put a down payment on a nice little condo. She'd fought the suggestion time and again. She loved this boat. She had redone the interior with a loving hand, turning it into a cozy retreat that had always felt more like home than her big, echoing minimansion back in Houston.

Most of her happy memories from her marriage had to do with the boat. She and Scott had sailed it all along the Texas coast and to Mexico. They'd gotten their scuba certifications and gone diving on every coral reef they could find within the boat's range.

Of course, all that was before Kaylee, back when Scott had still been trying to please her.

She took out her cell phone but hesitated before dialing. This was a big step. But then she remembered the look on Max's face, and imagined how he would feel if he could make his real-estate client happy by re-printing the magazines. That was worth more to her than clinging to a few memories that had passed their expiration date. She dialed.

Chapter Ten

"Max, I found someone." Carol stood at Max's office door. For two hours last night and an hour this morning, both of them had been on the phone, trying to find a printer that could do the job within the required time frame. "Sharp Printing in San Antonio. They have a narrow window on Wednesday they can fit you in, but you have to commit by noon today."

If Jane didn't come through by noon today, he was sunk anyway. She was noticeably absent from work, and Max had chosen not to call and check on her. He hoped—perhaps irrationally—that she was out doing something to raise the ridiculous sum of money he needed.

"How much do they want?"

Carol stepped into the office and handed Max a slip of paper with the quote on it. Max winced, though it was pretty much what he'd expected.

"Good work, Carol."

"I'm counting on someday getting a bonus. And a raise."

"Don't get your hopes up."

"Aw, come on, boss. We'll get through this. Every new company takes a few missteps."

"Not like this. I screwed up. I spent too much of my money on the office remodeling. I was sure business would come rolling in a lot faster than it has, and I didn't keep near enough money in savings as a contingency fund."

"We'll get through this," Carol said again. "Don't you have a bunch of rich relatives who would lend you money?"

"No way," he said automatically, because he had promised himself he would do this without any help from his family. He could just imagine how his brother would spin it. He would call it a bailout. He would turn it into a joke.

But so what if he suffered some humiliation? The alternative was to close his doors and put people out of work, people like Jane and Carol who really needed their jobs, and Finley, the account executive he'd just hired, the one who'd turned down another, less risky position because he'd been swayed by Max's enthusiastic forecasts for the future.

He reached for the phone just as Jane burst through the front door. "I got it. I got it!" She stormed through the reception area and nearly ran Carol over as she plowed her way into Max's office. "Max, if you'll come to Coastal Bank with me right now, we can set up a line of credit for ten thousand dollars with a whole lot more to come in five days."

Max was too stunned to speak.

Carol wasn't. "Get *out* of here. You are da bomb, girl!"

"Come on, Max." Jane came over and grabbed his arm, attempting to drag him out of his chair. "Did you find a printer?"

"We did," Carol answered. "Should I call them back, Max, and commit?"

"Jane, where did you get ten thousand dollars?"

"That's not your worry."

He was tempted, but only for a moment. "I can't borrow money from you." If he wouldn't borrow from his own family, how could he justify accepting money from his employee, a struggling single mom?

Jane looked crestfallen, but only for a moment. "Let's not call it a loan, then. I'm investing in the Remington Agency."

He shook his head. "I can't let you do that. Much as I want to believe this is only a temporary cash-flow problem, I can't guarantee a return on your investment."

"I don't need a guarantee. I believe in you."

He started to turn her down again. But then he saw something in her eyes, and he knew he couldn't. Jane wasn't just bailing him out. Keeping the agency afloat was important to her, personally.

Then there was Carol, staring at him with hope glowing from her face. How could he disappoint her, too?

"You understand that getting these magazines reprinted is only a temporary solution. I have a balloon payment on my business loan coming up next week."

Jane didn't seem fazed. "We'll deal with that when the time comes. Just take the money, okay?"

Max was out of his chair and across the office in two seconds flat. He scooped Jane into a bear hug. "I don't know what you did, or what I did to deserve having you come to the rescue, but thank you."

She returned the hug, and they probably held each other for too long, given that Carol was standing right there looking on with a knowing half smile.

With determined effort, Max withdrew from the hug. Jane was beaming up at him. "What next?"

"Carol, tell the printer they'll have files by the end of the day. Jane, you and I will go over the page files one more time and make sure everything's perfect, then we'll send them to the printers. On Wednesday I'll go to San Antonio to personally oversee the printing." He crossed his fingers. "Then this nightmare will be over."

MAX DIDN'T ASK Jane again where she'd gotten the money, for which she was grateful. He would have a fit if he knew she'd sold her boat. But the more she thought about it, the more she knew she'd made the right decision.

A boat was no place to raise a child. Kaylee was old enough now that locked doors wouldn't contain her for long. What if she wandered outside when Jane wasn't paying attention?

Kaylee needed a backyard to play in, or at least a neighborhood playground, and a neighborhood where there'd be playmates rather than rough dockworkers and fishermen.

With the proceeds from the sale of the *Princess II,* Jane could comfortably buy a two-bedroom condo or maybe even a little house. She'd seen several cute cottages in the real-estate magazine as she and Max went over the proofs.

"Let me fix the color balance on that picture," Jane said. She and Max were nearly finished going over the real estate magazine, sitting almost side-by-side at her computer. After an hour and a half of this, his nearness was getting to her. Every time he reached for the keyboard to move to the next page, his sleeve brushed her bare arm.

But nothing had been said about yesterday's incendiary kiss. She still didn't know how she felt about it, only that she'd been reliving it on a regular basis since it had happened.

She wasn't going to bring it up if he didn't. He'd probably put it behind him. He'd probably kissed three or four women since her.

Once they were done fine-tuning the magazine, Jane retreated to her office and worked on some sketches for another potential client, this one a chain of veterinary clinics. Sketching puppies and kittens relaxed her as nothing else could, and the day flew by. Again she was struck by how lucky she was someone would pay her to do this kind of work.

At five o'clock Max was engrossed in a phone call. Tomorrow he would be in San Antonio for most of the day. Some separation would do them good, Jane thought. She waved to Carol and slipped out the door.

When she arrived home a few minutes later, the *Dragonfly* was just pulling into its slip. "Hey, Janie!" Cooper called as he hopped onto the dock. "Hey, Flipper!"

Kaylee giggled as she always did when anyone called her that. Allie had christened her with that name because she swam like a dolphin, and it was catching on.

"Hey, Cooper," Jane called back. "Good day?"

"Better than good. Never saw so many fish. In fact, we were planning to ask you and Kaylee to dinner at the house on Friday for a fish fry. Sound good?"

Jane's mouth watered. Since she started working, she'd been subsisting on anything quick and frozen. "What time? I'll bring a salad and some bread."

When Friday rolled around, Jane was more than ready to forget about work and Max, and enjoy a relaxing evening with her friends. After work she quickly changed into shorts and a halter top, as the summer heat still gripped Port Clara despite the fact the calendar said it was late September. She grabbed some bagged baby spinach and a few other things from her fridge, as well as a bottle of wine she and Scott had bought months ago and never opened.

Kaylee was happy to be spending time with her mom and didn't much care where they did it, so they were both in high spirits as they drove up to Cooper and Allie's cute white brick house. Cooper had rented it a few months ago, but when the couple had gotten married, Allie had so fallen in love with the house that they'd arranged to buy it.

Jane loved it, too. It was nothing like the cold, contemporary house she and Scott had shared, nor the stiffly traditional home in which she'd grown up. Though it had half the square footage, it felt warm and welcoming.

Jane and Allie hugged just inside the door. "I'm so glad you came," Allie said. "What's the use of living by the sea if you don't have fish fries and invite all your friends?"

It quickly became apparent that this wasn't just a cozy dinner, but a party. Sara and Reece arrived, then some neighbors with a little boy just Kaylee's age.

Jane's happy, warm mood vanished when Max showed up—with a gorgeous, auburn-haired beauty in tow.

Allie ran to the door to meet them while Jane cowered in the living room. Oh, God, how was she going to handle this? She hadn't expected the surge of jealousy that welled up inside her at the sight of her boss with another woman.

Deep breaths. He didn't owe her anything, she reminded herself. Just because she'd *sold her boat* for him, just because two days ago he'd been so hot for her he hadn't been able to control himself, was no reason she should start thinking they shared something special.

It was better if he was interested in someone else. Her divorce was still so fresh; bouncing into another relationship, even a casual one, was a terrible idea. Yeah, she'd let herself fantasize about it, trying to justify the attraction that simply would not go away. She had told herself that maybe it could work if they were careful…

But it had all been a useless mental exercise, because here he was with this stunning woman who had a laugh like a chimpanzee—

"Jane?" It was Sara. "What's wrong?"

"Uh, nothing. Nothing." Deep breaths.

"You're hyperventilating. Something must be wrong."

"Fresh air." She turned and headed out the sliding glass door to the patio, where Cooper and Reece were debating how best to arrange the charcoal.

"Jane, you're all pale."

"It's nothing. I'm okay now." She forced herself to slow her breathing. Talk about an overreaction. She'd had no idea her feelings for Max were such a big deal, but apparently she'd been hiding them even from herself.

"You're not pregnant, are you?" Sara whispered.

That made Jane laugh. "Of course not!"

"I just thought…since you stayed at the Hotel Alexander with Max—"

"Nothing happened. I told you that. Anyway, even if it had, I'd hardly be having pregnancy symptoms yet. It's only been a week."

"It didn't take me long to notice something was up. Hey, look, I'm showing!" She raised up the hem of her shirt slightly to reveal a small baby bump.

Jane smiled, relaxing. "That's great, Sara."

"And I feel fantastic."

The sliding glass door opened, and Max stepped out, with the beautiful woman hot on his heels. Jane instantly tensed up again.

"Oh," Sara said with a knowing nod. "I see what's got you all discombobulated."

"What? What are you talking about?"

Sara rolled her eyes. "Give it up, babe. It's all over your face."

Hell. She was going to have to leave if it was that obvious.

Unfortunately, Max made a beeline for her. "Jane. Can I talk to you a minute? Oh, hey, Sara. It's about work. You don't mind, do you?"

Sara grinned. "Of course not."

The auburn-haired siren watched intently as Max touched a hand to Jane's back, right on her bare skin, and guided her away. She shivered from the roots of her hair to her toes.

"You're not cold, are you?" Max asked solicitously.

"No. Is something wrong at work?" Maybe she shouldn't just leave without telling him.

"Everything at work is fine. I just wanted to ask you, if you don't mind, not to mention our pink-magazine disaster to anyone else."

"I won't, of course. But why would you worry? From what I can tell, your cousins are completely supportive."

"Yeah, but not all of the family is. I just don't want it to get back to my brother or either of my parents that…well, that I let an employee bail me out."

"I won't say anything." She didn't really want it to get around that she was selling her boat, either. Cooper and Allie knew, but since Cooper was acting as her attorney, he wouldn't blab it to anyone.

"You look hot."

"A minute ago you thought I was cold."

"No, I mean…hell, what am I doing? I told myself I wouldn't do this."

Oh, now Jane got it. Duh. She looked *hot*. Her nipples tightened beneath her halter top, and she really, really wished she'd chosen a shirt she could have worn a bra with.

"Maybe you better get back to your date," Jane said primly.

"Who?"

Goodness, he had a short attention span. "The gorgeous, six-foot woman you arrived with?" She nodded toward the woman in question, who was staring holes through Max's back.

Max glanced over her shoulder. "Her?" He laughed. "I just met her."

"You work fast, then."

"No, I mean, I really just met her. We arrived on the front porch at the same time. She's Cooper's neighbor."

Jane's face grew even warmer, if that were possible. She had just made a complete idiot of herself. Worse, Max was no longer safely out of reach. He was a free agent.

She was in trouble.

"Are you jealous?" Max whispered.

"Stop flirting with me," she whispered back.

"I'll stop if you really want me to. So long as you know—anything personal between us has nothing to do with work."

That wasn't really her biggest concern. Yes, workplace romances could cause heaps of trouble, but she was more concerned about her heart. She wasn't just attracted to Max. She saw the potential for a deep emotional attachment, as well. And how could she trust her judgment right now?

He made her feel appreciated and valued, all the things she hadn't gotten from Scott. And he related well to Kaylee, also another of her ex's shortcomings. Her budding feelings for Max could be nothing more than a knee-jerk reflex.

"We shouldn't, Max. Really."

His mischievous grin disappeared. "Okay. Guess I'll have to flirt with Wendy."

"Wendy?"

He nodded toward the siren.

Jane's reaction was swift and instinctual. "Stay away from her. She's a barracuda."

Max's grin returned. "I like barracudas."

Just then something catapulted into Max's leg.

"Max!"

He looked down as Kaylee wrapped herself around his leg, and his grin widened. "Hey, there, Kaylee. Are you ready to eat some fish tonight?"

She nodded and held her arms out, wanting to be picked up, and Max obliged. Apparently she'd either forgotten or forgiven him for kicking Scott at the restaurant. Max hugged Kaylee and she hugged him back, her eyes squeezed shut as she reveled in the experience.

Jane watched with a lump rising in her throat. Scott had never hugged his daughter that way. The child was

starved for fatherly affection. Last weekend during his
visitation he'd barely spent any time with her, leaving
her with his parents while he partied.

But Max?

Why had Kaylee formed a bond with him so quickly? She'd spent a lot of time around Cooper and Reece,
both of whom had babysat, and she liked them fine. But
she had especially close feelings reserved for Max.

Maybe it was that overnight trip, when they'd
behaved so much like a family.

Kaylee had pretty much lost the only father she'd
ever known, a father she loved, as lousy as he was. Jane
was determined to prevent her daughter from forming
an attachment to Max, who certainly wasn't destined to
be around long-term.

That meant she had to keep Kaylee and Max apart.

Though it pained her to do so, she pulled Kaylee out
of Max's arms and set her on the ground. "Kaylee, your
new little friend looks lonely. Don't you want to play
with him? Why don't you two try out the teeter-totter?"

"Okay, Mommy." She dashed off, unconcerned, confident that Max wasn't going anywhere. How many dis-
appointments would it take before she would become
mistrustful, slow to give affection?

"She's a great kid," Max said.

"I know. I'm lucky. She likes you an awful lot."

"You say that like you think it's a bad thing."

She answered cautiously. "Kaylee's vulnerable right
now. She's anxious to attach to someone."

"And you don't think I'm the right someone."

This discussion wasn't going so well. She started to argue that she hadn't meant any slight, but he interrupted.

"It's okay, Jane. I know what you mean. She might have gotten the wrong idea in Houston."

"Exactly. I explained it as best I could, but she's too young to reason with."

"So you won't ever have another man around because you're afraid of disappointing Kaylee?"

She frowned. Single parents shouldn't be forced to isolate themselves just because they're afraid of disappointing their children. Yet...

"Okay, Max, let's just put it on the table. If you and I should, um, start dating, I know you and Kaylee would grow close. It's obvious. Then what if something happened and you suddenly disappeared from our lives? She's already so confused about her father's vanishing act—"

There, she'd said it. The worst was over. Now he knew how she felt, what she'd been thinking about.

"I understand. More than you know."

"So...we move on." She had to force the words out of her mouth. "If I ever get involved with someone else—and that's a big 'if'—it will be when I'm ready to settle down, and the man is, too. That doesn't describe you and me. I mean, I just got divorced and you...well, I've seen your little black book."

She held her breath, half hoping he would argue with her. And for a moment, he stared at her intently. But then suddenly he grinned. "You looked in my black book?"

So, he agreed. He wasn't the settling-down type. "Just by accident."

"I haven't put a girlfriend in there in months. Well, weeks, anyway."

"Slowing down, are you?"

His grin faded. "You don't have to put it like that. I've been too busy to date. No, that's not it," he quickly added. "Maybe I'm not ready to settle down. But since the day you walked into my office and strong-armed me into a job, I haven't been interested in other women. If I were, I'd be all over Wendy. Dating her would be easy—no complications.

"But I don't want Wendy. I want you."

Chapter Eleven

Max tried to swallow, but his mouth was too dry. Had he actually just said that? Had he thrown himself at Jane Selwyn, his employee and a freshly divorced single mom who was *not* interested in a casual relationship?

Yes, he had. He'd broken every rule he'd ever made for himself regarding women.

Max pinched the bridge of his nose. "Before you say anything, let me just make it clear that no matter how you react in the next thirty seconds, your job is completely secure. You could throw your drink in my face and I would still be happy to see you at the office come Monday morning."

At least she wouldn't have to worry about her job, which she seemed to do on a daily basis.

Her eyes widened slightly. "So despite everything I just said, you...uh..."

"I'd like to see you outside of work. Socially." Sexually. He trusted she understood that part without him spelling it out. "You can say no." *Please, don't say no.*

"It wouldn't be smart for either of us," she said a little desperately.

"So was that a no? One simple word, Jane, and you can easily put an end to this discussion. I'll never bring it up again."

She opened her mouth. But no words came out.

"Just think about it." He walked away while he was ahead.

JANE MANAGED to get through the fish fry with no further contact with Max. She took him at his word—she was going to think long and hard about taking the next step with him. No impulsive moves.

She had until Monday, anyway, before she saw him again. She spent the weekend quietly shopping for a new place to live. She'd thought she would probably go with one of the new beach condos. They were small, but they had ocean views.

Then the Realtor showed her a quaint little cottage. Well, not so little. Three bedrooms. It was in desperate need of paint and repairs. The kitchen was completely outdated, the tiny yard overgrown. But it had a big deck overlooking the dunes and the ocean beyond.

"I like this one, Mommy," Kaylee said as she stood at the railing, watching a trio of seagulls fly overhead.

"Really. What is it you like?"

"I don't know."

Funny, but Jane felt the same way. As dilapidated as the place was, it had a good feel to it. She could see it all fixed up, floors refinished, new furniture, a fresh coat of bright blue paint.

Of course, if she bought it, she wouldn't have any money left over for repairs. But the place was livable even without a makeover. She could work on it slowly, maybe finance the renovations with her portrait work. She'd been working like mad every evening, and she almost had enough finished drawings that she could send them to Erin Freeman.

She resisted the urge to sign a contract on the house. If she was being cautious about Max, she should be cautious about her new home, too.

JANE WAS STILL THINKING about both decisions Monday morning when she arrived at work bright and early. She immediately sensed a hushed tension in the office. Carol's brow was furrowed as she sat at her desk making notations on her computer. Max was in his office with the door closed. She could hear his voice on the phone, and he didn't sound happy.

She put her things away in her desk, then returned to the reception area. "Is something wrong? It's not the real-estate magazines, is it?"

"No, the client was thrilled and he actually wrote us a check on the spot."

"Then what's going on?"

"I'm not really sure." Carol took a sip of her coffee. "But I do know there's a loan payment due this week. Max has been counting on being able to put it off, even though Reece said no way."

"That's terrible." Jane would be crushed if her bailout only delayed disaster a few days. "How much are we talking about?"

"Again, I don't know for sure. But I overheard some figures being bandied about—we're talking mid-five figures, at least."

"Oh."

"The good news is, we have paychecks." Carol handed Jane an envelope. She peeked inside, a little disappointed in the amount. Still, it was her very first paycheck ever. She couldn't wait to show it to Kaylee.

Her first, and possibly last, paycheck from the Remington Agency.

A thought occurred to her. She would close the deal on her boat in a few days. She could invest the proceeds into the Remington Agency.

That would mean she couldn't buy the beach cottage. Her salary alone wouldn't qualify her for that high of a mortgage.

Was she crazy, even thinking about throwing away her entire divorce settlement, all so she could keep a low-paying job? But she believed in Max. Furthermore, she believed in herself. They could get things going, she knew they could. They just needed a little more time, and the cash would come rolling in.

Then Max would pay her back, and she could buy herself the beach cottage. Or a different one, if her first choice was no longer on the market.

Max came out of his office and joined them in the

reception area. He looked a little pale and not quite himself. "Good morning, Jane," he said with unusual formality.

"Hi. Everything okay?"

"Ah, not exactly. In fact, I'm afraid I have some bad news."

Carol put a hand to her forehead, as if she'd suddenly developed a killer headache. Jane just felt a dull ache in her stomach.

"I'm about to default on my business loan. The bank will start foreclosure proceedings, which means my operating accounts will be frozen. I'll have to close the doors. I'll try and come up with some severance funds for both of you—"

"No."

Max looked at her quizzically. "You don't want a severance check?"

"I don't want to be severed," Jane said. "Listen, Max—I can cover the loan payment. I think I can."

He shook his head. "I can't let you do that. It was bad enough, borrowing as much as I did—which I will pay back, by the way, I swear to you I will. But I can't let you throw any more money down a bottomless pit."

"It's not a bottomless pit. You're going to make it. I know you are. All you need is a few more weeks and you'll turn the corner, I know it."

"Jane. I appreciate your faith in me—"

"In me, too. I do good work. Look how happy Coastal Bank was with our presentation."

"Oh, yeah, they're thrilled, all right."

"Don't tell me they hold the loan."

"Uh-huh."

"Then they should understand we've got what it takes to succeed. Although it's probably a completely different department. Still…never mind. Tell me how much you need, and how much time that buys us."

"I can't let you—"

"Let her, for God's sake," Carol said. "I need this job."

"Jane, if you have all this money lying around, why were you so desperate for me to hire you?"

"It's a recent windfall. That's all you need to know. If you don't let me help you, I'll just march right over to Coastal Bank and handle it myself."

By noon, it was a done deal. She had backed Max into a corner, she knew, but in the end he'd grudgingly agreed to let her make the loan payment, buying them three whole months.

In three months they could conquer the world.

As they walked out of the bank, she was trembling. Had she completely lost her mind? If her parents got wind of her recent actions, they might just take steps to have her committed.

"Max, I need the rest of the afternoon off." She needed to start all over in finding a place to live, this time looking for a cheap rental. "Is that okay?"

"Yeah, of course. You want me to drop you off at the marina?"

She nodded.

They were silent as they settled into Max's Corvette, fastening seat belts. Max adjusted his mirror. "Second thoughts?"

"No," she answered without hesitation. "I know I did the right thing."

"I can't even begin to thank—"

"No, don't go there. My motives are purely selfish. I love my job and I don't want to lose it."

He put the brakes on, halfway out of his parking space. "Really? I thought I was a pretty horrible boss."

"No, you aren't. You work me hard. You challenge me to be my best. I need that."

"I pressured you to lie to a client. I forced myself on you in the break room."

She had to laugh at that. If that kiss involved any force at all, she was Angelina Jolie. "I guess I needed that, too."

He finished backing out of the parking space, unable to conceal the half smile on his face.

Jane felt warm all over just remembering that kiss. How had her life gotten so complicated? When she was married to Scott, she essentially had no choices except for whether to stay or leave. Now that she was single, her life was a mass of crazy decisions and complex, multilayered situations. Nothing was black and white anymore.

They were driving down Front Street, Port Clara's main drag, when Max's cell phone rang. He answered it, and Jane clicked her tongue and shook her head. She'd lectured him before about the dangers of driving and cell phones.

"You're kidding." He slammed on the brakes and stopped in the middle of the street. "You're kidding," he said again. "You wouldn't kid about this, Carol, would you? I mean, you're not getting back at me for never cleaning out the coffeepot—"

Jane closed her eyes. Was Carol quitting? That would be terrible. She was a crucial component of the Remington Agency, not to mention that Jane now considered her a good friend.

When Jane opened her eyes, traffic was backing up behind the Corvette and people were starting to honk.

"Max! You're blocking traffic!"

"Hold on, Carol, I have to drive." He set the phone in his lap and whipped onto the nearest side street, then pulled into the first available spot at the curb. "Okay, I'm back." He extracted a gold pen from his shirt pocket and searched for something to write on.

Jane pulled a notebook from her purse and Max scribbled something in it. "Okay. I'll call her right now...yes, I'll let you know." He disconnected, looking stunned and puzzled at the same time.

"Max, what is it? Have we had another disaster?" Another fiasco like the pink real estate magazine would finish them off.

"I don't know. Ellen Lowenstein wants me to call her."

"Really." That was interesting. "Do you know what she wants?"

"She wouldn't tell Carol. Maybe she plans to sue me for fraud or something."

"If she were going to sue you, her lawyer would call. Are you going to call her back or not?" Now Jane was consumed with curiosity.

"Carol said she seemed impatient to talk to me. That was why she tracked me down."

"Well, call her!" Then something occurred to Jane. "If you want some privacy, I can take a walk. I've been meaning to check out that quilt shop across the street."

"Don't you dare leave me alone. If it's bad news, I'll need you. If it isn't, I'll want someone to share it with."

Jane felt flattered that he would need her for anything. He'd always struck her as such a strong, self-sufficient man, though the events of the last week had shaken him, that was for sure.

"So, call her."

Max took a deep breath and dialed the number he'd just written down. His blood pounded in his ears. "Ellen Lowenstein, please. Max Remington, returning her call."

Ellen picked up almost immediately. "Max? How the heck are you?"

"I'm good. How are you?" he asked cautiously.

"I'm good, too. Listen, I've been thinking. And I don't like the way we left things."

"That makes two of us."

"It seems silly, now, getting our feathers ruffled over the fact you were pretending to be a husband and father. I mean, it's kind of flattering, the lengths you went to to get our business."

Max was afraid to say anything, so he didn't, but he reached over and grabbed Jane's hand, squeezing hard.

"I mean, even if you are a bachelor, clearly you like children and feel comfortable around them, and that's all I care about. What I'm trying to say is, I want you to do our advertising. None of the other agencies we talked to had your vision. And I want Kaylee to model for the magazine ads. Maybe the TV commercials, too."

Max thought his heart had stopped beating altogether. "That shouldn't be a problem." He was amazed he sounded halfway normal.

"I'm sending over a retainer check by FedEx. You should receive it tomorrow."

"Thank you, Ellen." He forced himself to breathe as they worked out the details of their next meeting, during which they would outline the specifics and sign a contract.

When he hung up, he realized he was still holding Jane's hand—nearly crushing it. He loosened his grip but didn't let go altogether.

"You got the Kidz'n' Stuff account?" Jane said.

"Yes."

Jane squealed and threw her arms around him, though it was an awkward hug in the Corvette's close confines. "I'm so happy for you! Your first national ad campaign."

"*Our* first. Your drawings are what tipped the scales." He didn't let her go, because it just felt too good holding her. She didn't seem eager to escape, either.

Suddenly they were kissing like mad, making out in his front seat like teenagers necking on a lovers' lane, except they were in the middle of town in broad daylight.

Max's body ached for more. "It's a good thing I don't have a backseat," he murmured against her ear.

He expected her to laugh, but she didn't. "My boat is five minutes away." She kissed him again, harder this time.

"So's my condo." He barely breathed the words.

"We can't. It's the middle of the day."

"Is that all that's stopping you?" More. He needed more of her. He buried his face in her soft hair and breathed in the scent. "We have to take a lunch hour."

His cell phone rang.

Jane pulled away. "Get it. What if it's important? What if you'd ignored that last phone call?"

He saw from the Caller ID that it was Carol. "What?"

"What happened?"

Oh, right. He was supposed to have called her. "We got the account." The triumphant feeling returned, surging through his body and mixing with his lust for Jane, transforming into a potent mixture.

"Oh, my God!" Carol screamed. "That's great! We need to have a party. Can I plan a party? I'm great at parties."

"As long as it doesn't cost me anything," Max said with a laugh. "Listen, I'm going to lunch. I'm turning my phone off. I'll be back by one-thirty."

"Okay, see ya then."

He turned his phone off and looked at Jane, who was studiously repairing her lipstick in the rearview mirror. "Change your mind?" he asked.

She looked at him, raising one eyebrow. "Did you?"

"Are you kidding? I just bought us—" he looked at his watch "—an hour and fifteen minutes."

Jane looked like she was about to burst. "What are you waiting for? Drive."

Chapter Twelve

Max turned the key. "Where to?"

"Your place." She didn't want to make love with Max on the *Princess II,* where memories of Scott might intrude. "My bed is tiny."

Jane applauded Max's control. He didn't break any speed limits driving to the Shell Beach Condos. But he didn't dilly-dally, either. After whipping into a parking space, he was out of the car and opening her door before she could even get her seat belt off.

They practically sprinted to the front door. Max opened it, punched in the security code to silence the beeping alarm, and before she could take a breath he had her up against the closed door.

He could take her right here on the tile floor and she wouldn't object. She'd never been so hot for any man.

With Max's help, she shed the silk blouse and tailored skirt she'd so carefully chosen this morning and threw it on the ground. Standing there in her plunge-front bra, high-cut panties, stockings and heels while Max's gaze devoured her only made her hungrier.

"Bedroom's this way." Rather than waiting for her to follow, he scooped her up and carried her up the stairs like some medieval maiden about to be ravished by the castle laird.

The image made her shiver with anticipation. In fact, pretty much everything increased her eagerness—the cool air-conditioning on her bare skin, the sight of his enormous bed, the faint traces of his scent on the pillow as he set her down on soft, cotton sheets.

He yanked off his dress shirt while she worked on his belt buckle, but he didn't need much help from her. In seconds he was down to his silk boxers, but she had only a moment to admire how he looked in sexy underwear before he shed those, too, and he was standing before her gloriously naked and awesomely aroused.

As he climbed into bed with her and covered her body with his, Jane reveled in the exquisite contact of hard muscles against her softer flesh. He radiated heat and desire, and his gaze burned with intensity as he stared into her eyes.

"You really are the most beautiful—"

"Yeah, you, too," she said distractedly as she unhooked her bra. She wanted his hands on her breasts. His mouth on her breasts. His mouth everywhere, oh, yes. No need for pretty words.

He slid her panties off with deliberate slowness, grazing his fingers along her bare thighs as he removed the wispy garment, making her whimper with wanting. He slid off her heels, too, but he left her thigh-high stockings on.

She was coming unglued. If she didn't have him inside her in the next ten seconds, her whole body was going to go up in flames. She beckoned him to her, grasping his muscular hip with one hand and his beautiful arousal in the other as she opened herself to him.

"Wait, honey, wait."

"Wait?" Did he have no idea how desperate he'd made her?

But then she realized he was reaching for the bedside drawer. He was thinking about protecting her, and all she could think about was getting her satisfaction.

Thank goodness one of them had a shred of sanity left.

He took care of that little detail in one smooth movement, no fumbling, which reminded her that Max wasn't exactly inexperienced when it came to women. The image of his little black book sprang to her mind for just a moment, but she banished it.

Who cared about the past? Or the future, for that matter. Max was here and now, and in moments he was going to be inside her and she was positive it would be the best thing that had ever happened to her.

Max resisted the urge to just dive into Jane's luscious body. He'd dated a lot of women, gone to bed with quite a few, too. But none had made him feel like this, like he wanted to sip and savor and create an experience that would live in their memories forever.

Moments ago he'd been in a rush. He couldn't get her or himself naked fast enough. But now that they were committed, he wanted to take it slower, to look and touch and taste.

"Max?" Jane asked a little desperately, and he realized he'd gone still while poised above her and was just looking, taking it all in.

He leaned down and kissed her, hoping she could feel even a fraction of what he felt right now.

Again she opened herself to him, and this time Max accepted the invitation, taking it slow, letting her grow accustomed to him. Every time he moved she made a little noise in the back of her throat, like a wild creature. The sounds only inflamed him further.

When he was perilously close to losing control, he plunged all the way in.

"Ah, yes, finally," Jane said, and he smiled, thinking she probably hadn't meant to speak aloud.

His movements steadied into a rhythm. Jane met him thrust for thrust, her eyes open and gazing into his, trusting, giving, generous. He pressed his cheek into her hair, inhaling the intoxicating fragrance as he tried to make it last.

"Oh…oh…" She seemed to hold her breath, then looked almost surprised as the spasms overtook her body, taking them both over the edge of sanity to a place Max had never been before.

Max rode the crest of the wave for what seemed like an eternity. By the time it was over and they lay together, limbs entwined, sweaty, her hair in glorious disarray, Max wasn't sure how much time had passed. He discreetly glanced at his bedside clock and was amazed they still had thirty minutes left of their lunch hour.

He fingered a strand of her hair, then tickled her nose with it. "Wish I could lie in bed all day with you."

"Mmm."

"On the other hand, showering with you would be nice."

Finally she opened her eyes, looking a little dazed. "That was crazy good, wasn't it?"

He laughed. "I'd say so. Maybe even worth the possible lawsuit."

She frowned. "Lawsuit?"

"When you sue me for sexual harassment."

"Oh, Max." She pulled her hair out of his hand. "You know I would never do that, right?"

"Sure, you say that now, when everything's all rosy."

She sat up and thumped him with a pillow. "Stop it. I'm not the suing type. I'm going into this knowing there might be consequences. What happens, happens."

"So what is 'this'?"

"What? What's what?"

"You said 'I'm going into this…' and I want to know what you think we're getting into."

"Jeez, Max. If you don't know, I certainly don't. It's a thing."

"A thing?"

"A hot, sexy, what-the-hell-are-we-doing thing."

"Is it a continuous thing?"

She grinned mischievously. "I don't know. Is it?"

He grabbed her shoulders and pinned her down on the mattress. "I hope you didn't do this just to satisfy an itch.

I sure didn't." Then he kissed her, just to make sure she knew he meant what he said. "I'm not ready for marriage. The agency has to be my priority for a few years. But that doesn't mean I want this to be a one-night stand."

"One-lunch-hour stand."

"Jane…"

"Sorry." She maneuvered herself away from him, and suddenly she did look serious. Almost too serious. "I don't want this to be an isolated incident, either. But I understand about priorities. I'm not one of those single moms shopping for a daddy for her kid."

Max hated hearing his words thrown back at him. "I never imagined you were."

She sat up, wrapping the sheet around herself. "Just one other small matter, Max."

"What?"

"I think…while we're figuring this thing out…you shouldn't spend a lot of time around Kaylee."

The thud of disappointment in his chest seemed all out of proportion. He rolled back onto his own pillow. "Oh."

"It's all that stuff we talked about at the fish fry. She'll get too attached, and—"

"You don't have to go over it again, Jane. I really do understand."

"Really?"

"Really. I had another little girl get attached to me once. Her name was Hannah."

Jane said nothing.

"As uncool as it is to bring up old girlfriends when

you're in bed with the new one, I'll tell you anyway. Her name was Alicia, and we were together a couple of years."

"You stayed with a woman for *two years?*"

"I know everyone thinks I'm some kind of womanizer, and maybe that's what I became. But I was happy with Alicia. Satisfied. She offered me something that was sadly lacking in my life, and that was a family. You know, that warm, family thing?"

"But you have a family."

"My parents got divorced when I was five. My mother had a string of boyfriends, even married a couple, but they never lasted. My dad had a couple more marriages, too. Eddie and I got bounced back and forth between them like ping-pong balls."

"Oh, Max, I'm sorry."

"Alicia was nurturing and warm, and she was a great mother to Hannah. And Hannah—what a great kid. The two of them made me feel I belonged in a way I never had before."

"And yet something went wrong."

"Alicia wanted more from me than I could give. She wanted marriage, and I wasn't ready. I was only twenty-eight, still focused on my career and hanging out with friends. And I didn't love Alicia. I wasn't in love with her, I mean. Looking back, I think I stayed with her as long as I did because I cared about Hannah, not because of Alicia. All in all, I was pretty selfish. I wanted what they could give me, but I didn't want to provide what Alicia needed."

"We all make relationship mistakes."

"And sometimes we hurt people in the process. I devastated Hannah when I broke up with her mother. She'd never even known her real father. I was the closest she'd ever had."

Max turned over to face Jane. He pulled her down and into his arms, because he couldn't stand not touching her. "I don't want to hurt Kaylee that way. She's a great kid, and I like being around her. She's like…sunshine.

"But I think you're right. I think I should keep my distance."

"And what about at work? Do we just act like before? Keep it secret?" She pulled the sheet up over her face. "Oh, God, I can't believe we're having this conversation."

"At work, of course we behave like professional colleagues." He hooked his finger on the edge of the sheet and pulled it down. "What's wrong with this conversation?"

"We're setting up the rules for a…a thing. Doesn't that strike you as odd?"

"Better than misunderstandings and fights and tears down the road," he said reasonably, which didn't seem to comfort Jane a great deal.

JANE WAS STILL a seething mass of conflicting emotions as she arrived for work the next morning. She was excited and terrified, happy and terrified, aroused at the mere thought of seeing Max…and terrified.

Mostly terrified that she'd done something incredibly stupid. And yet…she was glad she'd done it. No regrets. Just terror.

Carol greeted her with a smile. "Morning, Jane. Where were you all afternoon?"

"Oh, I had some personal business to take care of. Stuff left over from the divorce." Like not having a place to live.

After hours of slogging around in the muggy heat looking for a suitable apartment, Jane had finally found one she could stand. It was almost within her budget and not too vile. It was tiny, but then again, she and Kaylee were used to close quarters.

One small hitch, though. She couldn't move in until mid-October. And she had to turn over her boat to the new owners next week. That left her with almost two weeks with no roof over her head.

"So you heard the big news, yes?" Carol said.

"Yeah, I was there when Max talked to Ellen. It's great."

"It's fantastic. We don't have to go job hunting! I'm planning a party. It's tonight after work, can you come?"

"Oh, I'd like to, but I'd have to find a sitter for Kaylee." Hard to do on such short notice.

"You could bring her along."

"We'll see." But no, because Max would be there. She felt terrible, deliberately keeping Max and her daughter apart when they were so clearly crazy about each other. But after her conversation with Max yesterday, it only made sense.

She'd seen the pain on his face when he talked about Hannah. She didn't want to be the cause of something like that. And clearly their "thing" did not have a high chance of survival, not when she and Max were so not ready to make any commitments.

Jane was sifting through some mail that had arrived for her—amazing how quickly art-supply companies had pegged her as a potential customer—when Max walked in.

"Carol, have you talked to—oh, good morning, Jane." He had a big silly grin on his face, and Jane was afraid she had one to match.

"Hi."

"Uh, Carol, do you have the, uh…what did I come in here for?"

"Have I talked to…" Carol parroted his words back to him.

He snapped his fingers. "Right. Finley, the new account exec. He was going to call in with some information for payroll."

"Got it right here."

Jane slipped past Max and practically sprinted for her office. Being around Max and acting strictly professional was going to be harder than she'd thought. But she had to. It would look really, really bad for everybody to know he was sleeping with his art director.

She had a pile of work waiting for her, mostly small ads that needed minor updating. She put her purse away and fired up her computer, intending to make up for the time she took off yesterday.

Midway through the first ad, though, Max came into her office to discuss one of the projects.

Her mouth watered just looking at him. He was

casual today, and he looked better in a pair of faded jeans than any man she'd ever seen.

Their conversation was strictly business. Anyone seeing them or overhearing them would think nothing of it. But as they both bent over the ad on her drawing board, she could smell his soap—the same soap she'd used in his shower yesterday when he'd sudsed her up and done unspeakably wicked things to her body, causing him to be late returning to work.

Her whole body tensed with longing.

No. She was not going to give in to it. She had to focus on her work, because now she *really* needed this job. She'd forked over almost all her ready cash for the deposit and first month's rent on her new apartment.

Once the newness of sex with Max wore off, she wouldn't feel like this all the time, she reasoned. She would be able to partition off that part of her life.

"So, we're squared away on the surf shop ad?"

"Yes, mm-hmm."

"Something wrong?"

"No. No, everything's great." Sort of.

"Are you coming to the party tonight?"

"If I can get a sitter."

"You can bring—" He stopped himself. "Right. I hope you can make it, since you were instrumental in landing the account."

"I hope I can, too." Mrs. Billingsly sometimes did evening babysitting. Jane made a mental note to call her. "Where is this party, anyway?"

"On the *Dragonfly.* What's the use of owning one-sixth of a fishing business if I can't get a free charter now and then? Sara is doing the catering for the cost of food. We'll fish for a couple of hours in the bay, then anchor and eat and drink until the refreshments run out. If it's dark by then, we'll look at the stars through Cooper's telescope."

"It sounds like fun. I'll try to make it."

Carol leaned her head in the door. "Hey, girlfriend, I'm headed to Fresco Deli for lunch. You in?"

Jane took stock of her work and decided she had everything under control. "Sure."

"How about you, boss man?" Carol asked.

"I have some work to do. But if you could bring me back a ham and swiss on rye with mustard, I'd be grateful." He handed Carol a ten.

"Um, this is a health-food place. I could probably manage tofu and avocado on seven grain."

He grimaced. "Whatever. God, I miss New York sometimes."

It was a gorgeous day. The lingering summer heat and humidity had finally broken, and Jane inhaled deeply as she and Carol exited the building.

"Why don't we walk?" she suggested as Carol pulled her car keys out of her purse. "It's only a few blocks."

Carol shrugged. "Okay. I guess it is the perfect day for it."

They walked in companionable silence for about half a block, until finally a question burst out of Carol. "So? Are you going to tell me?"

"Tell you what?" Jane asked warily.

"About you and the boss man."

"What are you talking about?" Jane asked to buy herself time. Oh, dear, this was bad. It hadn't even been twenty-four hours since Jane and Max had succumbed to temptation, and already Carol knew about it.

"Come on, girlfriend. It's all over your faces—both of you. When he walked into the room you stared at each other like a couple of lovesick calves."

"Um…I plead the Fifth." What else could she say? Denials seemed ridiculous, and anyway she didn't like lying.

"Hah! I knew it! From the moment you first walked into the office I sensed a vibe between you two. C'mon, give. What's going on? Is he as hot as he looks?"

Jane shot Carol a sharp look.

Carol rolled her eyes. "He's not my type—too young, too scrawny and too pale. But I recognize prime beef on the hoof when I see it."

Jane gave an embarrassed laugh. "Carol, please."

"You did it at lunch yesterday, didn't you? Max came back to the office looking like he was going to burst, he was so happy."

"Of course he was happy. He'd just gotten the Kidz'n'Stuff account."

"You're evading the question."

They'd arrived at the deli, and Jane busied herself studying the menu as they stood in line at the counter. "They have a ham and swiss," she said.

"I know, I just said that to jerk Max's chain. He's always talking about how great the delis are in New

York. Interesting that the first thing you looked for when you picked up the menu was something for your man."

"Carol, *stop it.*"

"If you want me to stop it, you gotta come clean. If you and the boss man are steam-pressing the sheets, it could cause problems. I need to know the truth, so I can commence damage and rumor control."

Jane thought that was a pretty thin excuse for simply wanting to hear gossip.

"I'll tell you," Jane finally said.

She waited until they'd both picked up their sandwich orders and taken them to a small table on the sidewalk outside. Carol watched her with curious eyes, but she didn't push further.

"We slept together one time. It was at his place, yesterday, and I have no idea where it's going or even *if* it's going. It might be that we got it out of our systems."

In a way Jane wished that were the case. But Max certainly wasn't out of her system.

"Hmph, I doubt that." Carol took a bite of her turkey sandwich. "So what's his place like?"

Jane hadn't been paying much attention to Max's condo at the time, because she'd been way too focused on other things. But now that she thought about it, she had some recollections. It was big. Two stories, probably three bedrooms. And it was fancy. Modern furniture, but good quality. Nice rugs. Nothing cluttered or fussy.

Still, she thought sharing details about Max's home

bordered on gossip. "Do you want your pickle?" She nodded toward Carol's plate.

"Okay, I get it. You aren't into sharing details. I can accept that. But just answer me one thing. Do you *want* it to get serious? 'Cause you could do a whole lot worse than Max Remington. His family is worth millions. Some day he'll inherit. You could send Kaylee to Harvard."

"Carol. I'm not attracted to Max because of his money."

Or was she? One of the reasons she'd married Scott was because he was wealthy. She wouldn't have admitted it at the time, but in the back of her mind she'd known that as his wife she wouldn't have to worry about money.

Was she doing the same thing now? She was scarcely away from one rich husband. On some level, was she counting on Max to someday be Rich Husband #2?

Chapter Thirteen

Max reached into Sara's Tupperware, grabbed a stuffed mushroom, and popped it into his mouth.

"Hey, let me at least get them onto a platter." They were setting up refreshments on the *Dragonfly* in preparation for the first Remington Agency party. Carol was already there, and the others—his two account executives, Jane and Reece—would arrive soon. Cooper and Allie were readying the boat for a leisurely cruise around the bay.

"These are good." Max reached for another mushroom, but Sara batted his hand away.

"No more. Give the guests a chance at the food, please. You know, Reece claims that when you were kids and you stayed at his house, if there was something on his dinner plate he didn't like, he would slip it to you or the dog."

He laughed, feeling happy and relaxed for the first time in a good while. "True. I'll eat anything."

A movement on the *Princess II* next door caught his eye, and his heart did a flip-flop as it always did whenever he saw Jane. She opened the hatch and stood in the doorway, barefoot but otherwise still in her work clothes.

Max stepped to the railing and waved. "C'mon over. We can start the party any time now." He'd hardly seen her all day. He'd been taking around his new account exec, introducing her to clients he'd assigned her to, so he was looking forward to a few relaxing hours away from phones.

Not that he could touch Jane or kiss her or do any of the things he'd been constantly thinking about. But just having her near would be better than no Jane at all.

"I can't come," she said.

"What?"

"I couldn't get a babysitter."

Sara came to the railing. "You have to come. Why don't you bring Kaylee with you?"

Jane shook her head. "That's not a good idea. This is a grown-up party."

Now Allie joined the conversation. "C'mon, Jane. You know Kaylee's welcome. If you're worried about her safety, she'll have several worrywarts watching over her. I even have a safety line we can attach to her life jacket—"

"No, it's not that. I appreciate the offer, but I think we better just stay home tonight."

Max knew why she didn't want to bring Kaylee, so he didn't try to cajole her into coming, though he would feel her absence every moment.

Getting together with her was going to be something of a problem, he realized. Babysitters were expensive and unreliable, and he knew Jane wanted to spend her evenings with her daughter.

Maybe later, after the party and after Kaylee went to bed, he and Jane could go up on deck…and what? Would he forever be limited to clandestine meetings in the dark, stolen kisses, an occasional lunchtime tryst? That wasn't what he wanted.

He wanted to shout from the rooftops that Jane was his, which was ridiculous.

Now Carol joined in the conversation. "Jane, I'm coming over there to get you. You better be changed into your sailing clothes when I get there, too."

Ten minutes later, Carol had succeeded in dragging Jane and Kaylee to the *Dragonfly*. Jane looked incredibly sexy in her little white shorts and flowered T-shirt, her hair pulled back in a ponytail, though Max didn't think she had intentionally dressed to seduce him.

Kaylee made the rounds, hugging every adult who showed her any interest. Max attempted to stay in the background, which wasn't easy on a small boat, and when she inevitably saw him she ran toward him with arms outstretched.

"Max!"

What could he do? He wasn't going to snub the child. "Hey, Flipper." He gave Kaylee a brief hug, which was hard to do given her bulky life jacket. So he ruffled her blond curls, too.

Max expected Kaylee to move on, but she grabbed on to his hand. "I want to sit at the front."

Jane had joined them, looking troubled. "Kaylee, I bet Allie would let you sit up on the bridge with her."

"No, I want to sit in the front. Max, you come with me."

"Max has things to do, sweetie," Jane said. "This is his party, and he has to take care of his guests."

Kaylee pulled on Max's hand. "Come on, Max."

Max shrugged helplessly, and Jane looked resigned. "Fine."

The rest of the guests arrived, and Max greeted them all and invited them to eat and drink and make themselves at home. But as the *Dragonfly* got underway, he took Kaylee to the bow as she wanted. He enjoyed watching the little girl stand with the wind in her face, so filled with passion for life and that live-in-the-moment joy that only kids seemed to have.

Jane was watching, too, making sure Max had a firm grip on her little girl's life jacket. But she didn't seem worried. Kaylee knew her way around boats and wasn't about to do anything risky.

"I'm glad you came," he said to Jane. "I'd have missed you."

Jane offered a small smile. "I confess, when I thought I was staying home tonight, I felt really left out."

"Sorry about…" He tilted his head toward Kaylee. "I know this is exactly what you don't want to happen."

Jane sighed. "I can't control how she feels about you."

"Or how I feel about her, for that matter." At her worried look he added, "It'll be okay, Jane."

She nodded without much enthusiasm. "I'm sure you're right."

"Can I see you later?"

She shook her head. "No babysitter, remember?" She laughed. "There's a reason you don't date single moms."

"You know that's not the reason. After Kaylee goes to bed. We could sit out on the deck and just talk."

She looked surprised. "You'd be happy with that?"

"I like talking to you. I'd be happy." He leaned over to whisper in her ear. "Of course, the whole time I'd be thinking about making love to you. But sex is only a part of it. I'm not that shallow, despite appearances."

Jane blushed to the roots of her hair. "I never thought you were shallow."

Carol appeared with two pink, icy drinks. "Here you go, strawberry daiquiris. For the lovebirds," she added in an exaggerated whisper. Then she giggled and disappeared again.

"Did you tell her?" Max asked. It wasn't an accusation, but he'd known since yesterday that Carol somehow knew. "It's okay if you did. I'd rather her know the situation than speculate."

"She knew without me telling her anything. Apparently it shows on our faces."

"Oh." Max supposed he shouldn't be surprised. He always felt a little out-of-control in Jane's presence.

"We may not be able to keep it private, you know. Lots of people have office…secrets, but everybody knows. At least, that's what Scott once told me."

"I don't care, Jane." And he realized he didn't. "If

people want to criticize me for…well, you know, they can just go right ahead."

"But what if it hurts your business?"

"How could it?"

"Mommy!" Kaylee broke in. "Look, dolphins!"

Sure enough, a pod of dolphins swam beside the boat so close he could almost reach out and touch them. They looked like they were playing tag, jumping in and out of the water, sometimes becoming completely airborne.

"Wow!" Max was almost as excited as Kaylee. He'd never seen them so close before. "I think they're putting on a show for us, Kaylee."

She nodded, her eyes bright, and Max felt a lump in his throat that was becoming familiar. How could Scott have just walked away from such an amazing little person? Even as he thought this, he knew it was too late to stop the bond forming between himself and Kaylee.

Not unless he kept away from Jane altogether, and how was he going to do that? He'd been with her one time, but now she felt as essential as life itself.

JANE WAS GLAD she'd come to the party. A spectacular sunset had led into a dark, moonless night, perfect for stargazing, and Kaylee's delight at spotting Saturn's rings as she looked through Cooper's big telescope had been such a pleasure to watch.

Observing her little girl interact with Max had warmed Jane's heart, too. Although she'd been abandoned by her real father, Kaylee seemed happier than she had in months, and Max was one of the reasons.

Was it fair to keep them apart? Or would she be punishing both of them because of some nebulous fear about what might happen in the future?

She took a sip of her bottled water and gazed up at the starry sky. It was a night for lovers.

"Kaylee's gone to sleep," Allie said, claiming a deck chair next to Jane. "I read her a story, but she conked out after only a couple of pages. I put her in the V-berth."

"Thanks, Allie."

"No charge. I never realized how much I like kids until I started babysitting for Kaylee. It's good practice for the future, too."

Jane's jaw dropped. "Allie, you're not expecting, too, are you?"

Allie grinned. "Not that I know of." She dropped her voice. "But Cooper and I decided to try. I don't know how it will work, with the charter business and all, but we'll cross that bridge when we come to it."

Jane grasped both of her friend's hands. "Oh, Allie, I'm so excited for you. Work should never stand in the way of having a family, if that's what you really want."

"Hey, if we have a kid, at least you, me and Sara can trade off babysitting."

"It's a definite plus, having friends who are so generous as you and Sara have been."

"So you want to leave Kaylee here for the night?"

The possibility had never occurred to Jane, and she must have looked confused, because Allie hastened to explain.

"Cooper and I decided since it's a late night, we

would sleep on the boat like we did in the old days. We could watch Kaylee for you, too—that way you won't have to wake her up when we get back to port."

Jane was undeniably tempted. Not that she ever begrudged spending time with Kaylee, but she also occasionally needed grown-up time.

But then a thought occurred to her. "Did Max put you up to this?"

"Max?" Allie looked puzzled. "Why would he…" Then she gasped. "You and Max?"

Oh, hell. She'd given it away, and so easily.

"Uh…well…"

"I *knew* there was something going on with you two." Allie bounced up and down like a little kid. "That cinches the deal. Cooper and I will take care of Kaylee tonight, and you and Max can be alone."

"That's not…I mean, we haven't—"

"Cooper is going to be so happy. Now that he and Reece have discovered the joys of matrimony, they both think Max—"

"Whoa, stop right there. Slow down, Allie. I'll admit, Max and I have become more than friends. But you can't tell anyone. It's touchy—he's my boss. And Kaylee—we don't want Kaylee to know."

Allie looked puzzled. "Why not? The two of them are priceless together."

"That's just it. If they get too close and it doesn't work out—"

"Why wouldn't it work out?"

Jane let out an exasperated breath. "So many reasons.

Neither of us want Max to become a father figure to Kaylee because we don't want her hurt. Please, Allie, trust me on this one."

"Okay, sweetie." Allie gave her a hug. "But leave Kaylee with us for the night. At least take a night off for yourself. You work so hard. Have you found a place to live yet?"

"Yes, but I can't move in until October."

"You can stay in our spare bedroom…for as long as you need."

Jane was so lucky to have such good friends. Sara and Carol had both offered, too. "Thanks, Allie. All right, keep Kaylee for the night."

Allie clapped her hands. "Yes, I get to keep Flipper!"

"Be sure and lock the hatch—and take the key. She's very good with doors and latches."

Allie held up her hand. "I will, promise. Now, go find your guy and invite him over. He's yours for the night."

They reached the harbor a few minutes later. Max was helping Sara pack up the leftovers; Carol was picking up a few remaining plastic cups and empty beer cans.

"Your party was an unqualified success," Jane said to Carol, who beamed with pride.

"I told you it would work out. And I hardly went over budget at all."

"Yeah, we'll talk about that later," Max said, but his voice held more teasing than warning. It was good to see him so happy. Maybe the agency had turned a corner, and that worry line between his eyebrows would disappear for good.

"I can get the rest of this, Max," Sara said. "You should go home and get some sleep."

Not if Jane could help it.

The brazenness of her thoughts surprised her, but Allie was right—she did need a grown-up night, away from kids, some place where she could forget budgets and deadlines, where she could stop worrying about the future and live in the now.

Max must have sensed something was up, because he stopped in the middle of tying the top of a garbage bag and looked straight at Jane. "Where's Kaylee?"

"Asleep in the V-berth. Allie and Cooper have kidnapped her for the night."

He nodded. "Ah. Ahh." He leaned closer and whispered, "Do they know, too?"

Jane sighed. "Everybody knows, Max. And they all think it's just so cute." She rolled her eyes. Didn't Allie and Cooper remember how complicated it was for them to get together? And Sara and Reece—he had to change his whole life to be with her. But, no, both of her best friends were in newlywed la-la land.

Just because two people "looked cute" together didn't mean they could just live happily ever after.

"Stop obsessing," he said firmly. "So they know. That means we don't have to be secretive anymore."

"It also means Kaylee knows, or she will shortly."

"Kaylee? She's just a baby."

"A baby who picks up on everything. If everyone around us has sensed it, she has, too. Which might explain her attachment to you."

The *Dragonfly* had docked, and everyone was getting off. Max grabbed the garbage bag and quickly finished tying it closed. Reece and Sara were negotiating the gangway with Sara's many containers of food and utensils.

"My purse is below deck," Jane said. Then added cautiously, "See you in a few?"

He gave her a look that nearly ignited her on the spot. "Absolutely."

Struggling for breath, she went below to grab her purse. Allie was straightening up the galley.

"Thanks again," Jane said.

"My pleasure. But tomorrow I want details."

"Allie…don't say anything to Kaylee about me and Max. Okay?"

Allie smiled. "She already knows."

That was what Jane was afraid of.

The evening had cooled off, and she shivered slightly as she made her way down Cooper and Allie's dock to her own, wondering how long before Max returned to her. She could hear voices from the parking lot as people said their last good-nights.

As she turned the key to open the *Princess II*'s hatch, something moved in the shadows on deck. She gasped—until she realized it was Max. "You scared me."

"That's not the reaction in you I'm looking for." He pressed her shoulders against the still-closed hatch and claimed her mouth with his, after which nothing else seemed to matter. The keys dropped from Jane's limp hand, and she wrapped her arms around Max's firm body and gave in completely.

As Allie had said, Max was her man…for this night, anyway.

Max cupped her bottom with one hand while the other slid inside her shirt at her waist, caressing the bare skin on her back and sending delicious shivers reverberating through her body like ripples from a stone dropped into a still pond.

He tore his mouth from hers, breathing heavily. "Maybe we better take this inside."

"I dropped the keys." She almost sobbed.

"I'll find them." He lowered himself slowly to the deck, skimming her body with his hands as he went down, tracing his fingers down her bare legs and placing a soft kiss on her thigh before feeling around on the deck.

What if they'd bounced into the water?

"Got 'em."

Relieved, she stood aside and let him open the hatch. She walked down the three steps, her legs shaking. The hatch had scarcely latched behind them when she was in his arms again.

They started toward her cabin, leaving a trail of clothing as they kissed and caressed one step at a time, but they never actually made it there. Jane found herself on the sofa in the salon, but that proved too small and they ended up on the carpet.

She couldn't get enough of the feel of his skin and his hair, long enough that she could grab handfuls of it. He smelled like citrus and his skin tasted faintly of salt from being out on the ocean.

She tasted his ear, delighting in the way he squirmed.

But when he kissed her breast, circling her sensitive nipple with his tongue until it peaked, she was the one driven nearly out of her mind with wanting.

"Birth control?" she managed to squeak.

"Got it."

In the back of her mind she wondered why he was so well prepared when he'd had no idea they would be together tonight. Was he just optimistic that an opportunity would present itself? Or if things hadn't worked out in their favor, would he right now be at Old Salt's trying to seduce some other woman?

But she pushed those thoughts out of her mind. Tonight was about living in the moment, not worrying, and the moment was pretty darn good.

By the time Max entered her she was incapable of thinking about much else, anyway. She wanted to scream with passion and excitement and sheer exuberance, but because she didn't want to alarm anyone who happened to be out for an evening stroll on the dock, she limited herself to heartfelt moans.

When her feelings threatened to overwhelm her self-control, she pressed her face against Max's shoulder and cried out one last time as the intense pleasure reached its peak.

As she rode out the waves of sensation, reveling in the simple physical release, Max thrust inside her harder and faster until he, too, found release.

A few minutes later, the air conditioner kicking on brought Jane back to the real world, and the fact she was lying on the salon floor with a delicious man on top of her.

This was crazy. She laughed, because what else could she do when she realized they were complete lunatics?

Max rolled over and pulled her on top of him. "What's so funny?"

"Us. We couldn't even make it to the bedroom."

"I don't know about you, but I had a lot of suppressed lust built up. Watching you parading around in those little shorts—"

"I do not 'parade.'"

"You can't help it. Everything about you turns me on. Your smile, your knees, your collarbone. Even your fingernails." His smile faded. "Jane, I think…I mean, I don't know much about these things, but…"

"But what?"

"Oh, hell, nothing. I never used to worry about anything, and lately I've been one big tension knot."

She wanted to know what he was worried about. But she sensed whatever it was, pressuring him wouldn't get results. He would tell her if and when he really wanted her to know.

She pressed two fingers into each of his temples and gently swirled. "Tonight isn't about worry, okay? I've been doing my best not to think about the future. Not even tomorrow morning."

"I have to get up early."

"Me, too. Allie will probably bring Kaylee home around 7:30."

"I'll be gone by then. But that gives us—" he raised his left arm and pressed a button on his watch. A cool blue-green light briefly illuminated his face "—nine hours."

"Nine hours! That sounds like a lot."

"Unless you factor in sleep."

"Who needs to sleep?"

"Not me. But I wouldn't mind a bed."

Reluctantly, Jane eased her body off Max's and got to her knees, then her feet. She offered a hand to Max. "Bedroom's this way. But don't expect much. Everything's smaller on a boat."

Jane had always found the main cabin on the *Princess II* to be adequate for her needs. But when Max entered, his presence filled it so thoroughly she felt like they'd entered a hobbit house.

"Good thing I don't mind cuddling up with you."

Jane pulled back the covers and slid between the sheets, and Max joined her. He couldn't even stretch out all the way, but he didn't complain. He tucked her against him and idly caressed her breast, and she sighed.

She'd never known a human being could feel such contentment.

It was just sex, she reminded herself. But she'd never felt this way with Scott, who by comparison had been a rough and insensitive lover, more interested in conquering her than pleasing her.

Tentatively she touched Max, pleased that he responded instantly and amazed that she could want him again, already. At this rate, in nine hours they could make love nine or ten times. She suppressed a giggle.

He probably hadn't come *that* prepared.

Chapter Fourteen

The second time they made love was slower, almost drowsy. Max thought he'd appreciated every part of Jane before, but now he noticed more things about her. She made little whimpers low in her throat when he found just the right place; she had an adorable freckle right in one of the dimples above her bottom.

Now thoroughly sated, Max was content to watch Jane as she fell asleep. So much for staying up all night.

But he had no more condoms anyway.

This was the point where, with other women, he'd felt a strong urge to flee. He hadn't spent an entire night with a woman since his breakup with Alicia, and even with her he'd stayed only because she had pressured him about it.

He had absolutely no desire to leave Jane. In fact, he could have happily stayed here with her for days. It was so easy to put work out of his mind. They could sail the *Princess II* to some secluded harbor where even Cooper and Allie couldn't keep an eye on them, and live on love and vanilla wafers.

Was this love? When you were fascinated with everything about a woman, in bed and out, and you cared more about her welfare than your own, was it love?

He'd almost told her he loved her. But some small grain of self-preservation instinct, maybe only a holdover from his swinging bachelor days, had stopped him.

It would be bad to say it if it wasn't true. And what did he know about love? He only knew that he'd never told any woman he loved her before, not even Alicia. Love—real, true love—implied a future together. Commitment. Marriage.

He had other priorities right now. The Remington Agency was on the brink of turning a profit. He couldn't afford to get distracted, worrying about Jane and Kaylee and how to provide for their futures as well as his own.

It was too much.

But if he'd fallen in love with her, how did he undo it?

He fell into a troubled sleep. Jane nuzzled him awake at some point in the early morning hours, when it was still dark out, and though he was out of condoms they still managed to pleasure each other in mind-boggling ways.

When seven o'clock came, Max had to drag himself out of bed. Tempting though it was to invent some excuse for blowing off the whole day and spending it in bed with Jane, he could just imagine the gossip fallout.

Jane, however, still snoozed blissfully. Max took one look at the miniscule marine shower and decided to bathe at home. How did Jane live in such tight quarters? The *Princess II* was large compared to, say, the *Dragonfly,* but it was still cramped.

When he was dressed, he woke Jane with a light kiss but pulled back when she reached for him.

"No, no, gorgeous. If we even get started I'll never make my meeting in time."

Jane sat up, rubbing her eyes like a child. "Wow. What time is it?"

"Seven-fifteen."

"I can't believe I slept this late. I never sleep past seven."

Max grinned. "We didn't get much sleep last night."

She grinned back. "Good point." Then she frowned. "You're already dressed."

"I have to go. I'm not sure how long this meeting will last—it might be an all-day thing."

"You never told me who you're meeting with. Is it a secret?" Jane slid out of bed, and Max got a glimpse of her lush curves before she grabbed a silk dressing gown from a hook and wrapped it around herself.

"It's not a secret, exactly. It's my brother, Eddie. I'm not sure if he's here to spy on me, scold me or beg me to come back. But whichever, I figure I owe him the courtesy of a meeting."

"So bring him to the office. Show off what you've built."

"Maybe. We'll see how it goes." He looked at his watch. "I have to get going. You won't be late to work, will you?"

"Huh, not a chance. I don't want people saying I slept in because I was up all night boffing the boss. Even if I was."

She walked him up to the deck, and they paused at the railing for one last, lingering kiss.

"Hi, Max!"

Max and Jane sprang apart as they both searched for the source of the cheerful greeting. Then Jane saw it; Kaylee was at a porthole on the *Dragonfly,* waving at them and grinning from ear to ear.

OF COURSE, Jane was left to deal with the fallout alone. Not that she blamed Max; he'd warned her when she invited him to stay the night that he had to leave early. But that meant Jane had to answer Kaylee's thousand-and-one questions all by herself.

She showered quickly and dressed for work. By then, Allie had gotten Kaylee into her clothes and was ready to bring her home. They met on the dock for the handoff.

"She was no trouble at all," Allie said. "Such a little angel, and so cheerful when she wakes up. I fed her a waffle."

"Can you say thank-you to Allie for taking care of you last night?"

Kaylee hugged Allie fiercely. "Thank you." But then she turned back to her mother. "Where's Max?"

"He's gone home, sweetie," Jane said.

"Did he say thank-you that he got to spend the night with you?"

Allie snickered, and Jane shot her friend a warning look. "Yes, he did." There was no point in denying she'd had Max as an overnight guest.

"Did you give him a waffle?"

"Is that what they're calling it now?" Allie asked.

Jane decided she needed to leave before the conversation deteriorated any further. "We'll talk to you later, Allie," she said tartly as she took Kaylee's hand and made her escape.

"Did you give him a waffle, Mommy?" Kaylee asked as Jane washed the child's face and hands and got her into some clean clothes. No time for a bath, but she was marginally clean.

"No, I didn't have waffles."

"Did you give him cereal?"

"No, he didn't eat breakfast."

"Won't he be hungry?"

"I'm sure he'll eat something when he gets home."

"Where does Max live?"

"He lives in a condo. It's like our new apartment that we're moving to."

"Can we go there?"

Jane hedged. She didn't want to come right out and discourage Kaylee from her attachment to Max, because that might make her want it even more. "Maybe some time he'll invite us over and we can see it."

"Why doesn't he live here?"

Jane prayed for patience and guidance. "Because this is our home, and he has his own home."

"When we move to our new 'partment, will he live there?"

"No, it'll just be the two of us. Just us girls."

Kaylee frowned, and she wiggled her foot making it

nearly impossible for Jane to tie her shoe. "I want him to live with us."

Jane groaned inwardly. "He can't live with us, sweetie. He's not part of our family."

"Why not?"

"Because…because families are made up of mommies and daddies and children and…and…" Oh, God, how did she explain this?

"Max could be my daddy."

Oh, boy. "Kaylee, you already have a daddy." A rotten daddy, but Jane still hoped that Scott would straighten up and form a decent relationship with his daughter once the sting of the divorce had worn off. She wouldn't do anything to ruin that for the future.

"But my daddy's not here."

"True, but that doesn't mean he's not your daddy."

"Then I could have two daddies. Joanie at school has two daddies."

Ay-yi-yi. "Kaylee, please, can we talk about something else? Max is a good friend, and he's my boss, and we owe him a lot, but he's not your daddy and he doesn't live with us."

Kaylee's big blue eyes welled up with tears. "Why not?"

"Oh, baby." She gathered her little girl into a hug and squeezed her tight. "I know it's tough that we don't have a daddy living with us. But I'm your mommy and I love you enough for all the daddies in the whole world. A hundred daddies couldn't love you the way I do."

Jane braced herself for a tantrum, but it didn't come.

Instead, Kaylee cried quietly, almost silently, as if her heart had just been broken, and maybe it had been. Maybe she finally understood that her daddy wasn't coming back. Jane had thought her daughter's transition from two parents to one had gone a little too smoothly.

It was all Jane could do not to cry herself. Seeing her daughter skin a knee or bump her head was hard enough; Jane died a thousand deaths every time anything hurt her baby. But seeing her with her first real, true emotional hurt was almost more than Jane could stand.

By the time she arrived at the Montessori school, Kaylee had stopped crying, but she still looked and sounded sad and nothing Jane could say would cheer her up—not even promises to take her to her favorite pizza place.

Miss Martha, Kaylee's teacher, waved from the porch as Jane got Kaylee out of her car seat.

"Give me a hug, and I'll see you at five-fifteen at Mrs. Billingsly's."

Kaylee hugged her, but trouble still brewed in her eyes. "Mommy, will you ask him?"

"Ask who what?"

"Ask Max if he wants to be my daddy."

Now Jane's eyes did fill with tears. "I can't, sweetie. I know you don't understand, but the world just doesn't work that way. But he can still be your special friend."

Kaylee firmed her mouth in a mutinous line, clearly not buying the comfort Jane offered. She ran off toward Miss Martha without a backward glance.

Jane got back behind the wheel and moved the car forward, but she didn't go far. She turned onto the first quiet side street she saw and parked while she pulled herself together.

She spent several minutes parked there, working through every conceivable solution to this problem, and every time she reached the same conclusion.

This wasn't going to work. If she didn't want to disappoint her daughter over and over and over again, she was going to have to stop seeing Max.

It was best to find out now, she reasoned, before they'd gotten in too deep. But then she realized she was kidding herself. They'd been involved since the moment she'd walked into his office looking for a job—maybe from the moment he'd first flirted with her, earning Scott's wrath. Yes, they'd only recently consummated their feelings in bed, but that didn't mean what they had was slight or shallow.

She was already in deep. And she had to get out.

Not only was she losing Max, but she was losing her job, as well. Oh, Max wouldn't fire her. At least, she didn't think he would. But it would be too painful to continue working so close to him when she couldn't have him.

She would have to resign.

"EDDIE!" Max spotted his older brother at the baggage claim. They strode toward each other, shook hands in a contest of who could squeeze harder, then broke down and hugged.

"Man, you look great," Eddie said. "You got a tan!"

"I got that before I started the agency," Max said. "It's fading fast now that I'm working eighty-hour weeks."

"I hear ya." Eddie, dressed in perfect business casual, grabbed his leather clutch from the baggage carousel. "That's all. Where to first?"

Max thought it a little odd that Eddie was letting him call the shots. Normally Eddie was an in-charge kind of guy, scheduling his time down to the minute. Max half expected his brother to produce a typed itinerary and had rehearsed how he would insist that he had his own schedule to keep—meetings and obligations. Max was the in-charge guy now, and he wanted his brother to know it.

But Eddie didn't try to control anything. He followed Max to the parking lot, praising the mild weather, the beautiful flowers still in bloom, the palm trees, the scent of the ocean.

"You really did move to paradise," he said, almost to himself, as he wedged his bag behind the seats of Max's 'Vette.

"It wasn't paradise in the summer," Max added for the sake of argument. "It was hotter than hell, even with an ocean breeze. But the winters are supposed to be great. So where to? Your hotel?"

"I…I thought I'd stay with you."

"Hey, great. No problem." Another departure. Eddie hated bunking with relatives. He traveled a lot and was accustomed to first-class hotels with twenty-four-hour room service and a concierge.

Eddie grinned. "Let's get some breakfast, then. Take me to that greasy spoon you're always going on about."

"Old Salt's?"

"Yeah, that's it."

Max resisted the urge to ask who this man was and what he'd done with Eddie. Something was up, but Eddie would reveal it when he was ready. Max only hoped it wasn't some elaborate hoax to get him to come back home.

During breakfast, Eddie kept gazing out at the ocean, sometimes looking perplexed, and sometimes with a faint smile on his face. He probably couldn't imagine why Max had thrown away his six-figure income to run a small-potatoes agency in a Podunk town.

"So, are you going to show me your company?"

Max hesitated. While his agency was upscale compared to most businesses down here, it was almost laughable compared to the opulent Remington Industries headquarters in Manhattan.

But then he shrugged. He was proud of what he'd built so far, and he was just getting started. He had competent and loyal employees in Carol and Jane…ah, Jane.

Damn, he couldn't afford to think about her right now. He had to be on his toes. Eddie had an agenda, and Max wanted to step carefully so he didn't fall into any traps.

A few minutes later, as Eddie entered the reception room of the Remington Agency and looked around, Max watched his brother closely. He seemed to take in everything and was probably mentally calculating the cost.

Carol smiled serenely from her desk. "Good morning, Mr. Remington," she said in her most polite, obsequious voice for Eddie's benefit. She didn't know who Eddie was and assumed he was a client.

"Carol, this is my brother, Eddie. He's visiting from New York."

Carol stood and extended her hand. "Oh, now I see the family resemblance! How nice to meet you. Can I get you some coffee?"

Eddie took her hand and held her gaze for several seconds. He had the ability to make anyone he talked to feel like they were the most important person in the world. It was one of the things that had earned him his nickname, "The Persuader."

"No thanks, Carol. We just had breakfast."

"You let me know if you need any little thing."

Max rolled his eyes. "C'mon, Eddie. Let me show you the rest." Might as well get it all out in the open. The rest of the office was stylish but not nearly as impressive as the entrance.

"How many offices?" Eddie asked as they entered the hallway.

"Six. But I might be able to expand into the next office suite. Right now, though, this is fine. I have my office, Jane's, one for each AE and the media buyer, and a conference room."

"Who's Jane?"

The woman in question swung out of her office just then. "Oh, Max…"

Max made introductions, feeling unaccountably

uneasy. What, was he afraid Jane would fall for his brother? That was ridiculous.

"Well, hello there." Eddie flashed his trademark lady-killer smile, and Jane smiled back briefly and exchanged hurried pleasantries, but her attention returned immediately to Max.

"Max, I need to talk to you. Soon."

Uh-oh. That didn't sound good. "Is there a problem?"

"Yes, but—" she glanced at Eddie and smiled again, but it didn't reach her eyes "—it can wait."

"I trust your judgment. You handle it however you see fit."

"Buzz me when you're free." She slipped back into her office and shut the door.

Max's uneasiness grew, but he tried not to show it in front of Eddie. They went into his office, and he showed Eddie some of the agency's best work—Jane's work, mostly.

"This is good stuff. Who's your creative director? And where are the copywriters?"

"You're looking at him. For now, Jane and I handle all creative."

Eddie laughed. "You always did have a flair for that kind of thing. I can sell the hell out of anything, but I was never a concept man like you. So you're doing okay? Making money?"

Max had no reason to lie. Eddie had no power over him. "Haven't turned a profit yet, but I can see light at the end of the tunnel."

"Are you able to pay your people well?"

Max shook his head. "I'm paying them peanuts. Every one of them is taking a gamble on me and on the future of the Remington Agency."

"Jane's going to get stolen, you know," Eddie said. "Once her work starts getting national exposure, the headhunters will come calling."

"She'll stay," he said with more confidence than he felt. If she did get a better offer from some big agency, he didn't want to hold her back. "She likes working here and she likes Port Clara."

"Money talks, bro. If you want to keep her, and you can't pay her what she's worth, you should offer something else. Ownership incentive, maybe."

Max's first reflexive instinct was to balk at the idea. The Remington Agency was his and his alone. He'd hated accepting money from her, and he intended to pay it back at the first opportunity.

But then he reconsidered. Jane was already functioning as a partner. Their experience with Coastal Bank had taught him to trust her input in all matters, not just the artistic side.

Remington & Selwyn. That sounded nice. "I'll think about it."

"Good." But suddenly Eddie looked uncomfortable. He got up and closed Max's office door, and Max braced himself. *Here it comes.*

"Okay, so here's the deal. How would you like to be able to pay your people what they're worth, including yourself? How would you like to have a mammoth expense account? How would you like to expand into those offices now instead of later, hire the help you need, have any business resource at your disposal? How would you like a few national accounts thrown your way?"

Max had to laugh. Now he knew what was coming, and it wasn't the move he'd expected. "Don't tell me. Remington Industries wants to invest in the Remington Agency…in return for complete control."

"They want to buy you outright," Eddie said, sounding regretful. "You cannot imagine how it's gotten under Dad's skin, the fact you left and thumbed your nose at the company. At first he figured you'd fall flat on your face because you had no business sense. Then he thought you'd simply give up because you wouldn't be able to earn what you were used to."

"And now what's he saying?"

"Not much. He just handed me a blank check and told me to buy you out."

"A blank check, huh?"

"I only told you that because I know you'd never accept. I see it in your face and hear it in your voice. This agency is your baby, and you wouldn't give up any portion of control, not for any amount of money. Am I right?"

"You're right." If this offer had come last week, Remington Industries might have acquired itself a new subsidiary. But not today. "Dad needs to lighten up. He still has you."

"Huh, not for long."

"Excuse me?"

"I made you the offer and you turned it down. I've done my duty for the family corporation. But I came down here for another reason. Any chance you'd give your brother a job?"

Chapter Fifteen

"What?" Okay, now Max was sure he'd dropped down a rabbit hole. Was this some new ploy?

"Just give me a sales job. Straight commission is fine. I have contacts. I can get you some great accounts."

Max didn't doubt that was true, but... "Why, Eddie?"

"The situation at the company has become intolerable. Your contribution to the marketing department was grossly undervalued, and nobody seems to be able to take up the slack. Things are in chaos—and I've become the whipping boy in your absence. I think Dad figured if he bought you out, then pulled the plug, you'd be forced to come back.

"I can't work in that kind of atmosphere anymore," Eddie concluded. "I like it here. This place feels good."

"But you're gonna be a vice president someday," Max argued. "You'd be giving up literally millions of dollars. What does Rhonda say? What about the kids?"

"The kids' college funds are taken care of. As for Rhonda, she wants out of New York. She doesn't need much, never did. She would love it here."

Max could hardly believe his good fortune. Eddie was one of the best salespeople Max had ever met, in any industry. "When can you start?"

They worked out a few details and shook hands on it, after which Max was eager to share the news. Jane was the first person he wanted to tell. But when he checked her office, it was empty.

He checked the break room; she wasn't there, either. Maybe she was talking to Carol. But when he entered the reception room he didn't see Jane. Just Carol, looking fidgety and worried.

"Oh, there you are."

"Where's Jane?"

"She wanted to wait for you to get out of your meeting, but in the end she couldn't. She made some excuse…in fact, I think she said something about packing. If you two are taking another business trip, you might want to let me know."

Packing? That didn't sound good.

"Did I not tell you?" Eddie said. "It's too late."

Max's blood pounded in his ears. It couldn't be. She wouldn't accept another job. Of course she had to think about what was best for herself and Kaylee, but…no. He wouldn't jump to conclusions until he'd talked to her.

"She didn't look happy," Carol said. "You didn't do something to upset her, did you?"

As usual, Carol said exactly what was on her mind. "Not that I know of." Everything had been fine this morning, although Kaylee's untimely interruption hadn't sat well with Jane.

"Carol, Eddie's our new account executive. Give him all the appropriate paperwork, would you?" It wasn't how he wanted to make the announcement. But suddenly his priorities had shifted. "I have to make some calls." Or rather, one call. What had Jane wanted to talk about?

He stepped into his office and dialed Jane, first her cell, then her home phone. She didn't answer either.

Hell, Port Clara wasn't that big. He would just go find her. And he would make damn sure she wasn't tempted to sell out to the first fast-talking headhunter who crossed her path.

JANE SNIFFED BACK TEARS as she packed up her kitchen into cardboard boxes. She'd been putting this off. Since she wasn't fit to focus on artwork, and she couldn't possibly talk to Max while his brother was here, she'd decided it would be a good time to pack.

One nice thing about living on a boat—packing didn't take long. Most of her possessions—those few things Scott hadn't claimed—were already in storage.

The tears weren't because she was leaving the *Princess II* for good. She mourned the loss of a relationship that hadn't even really gotten started. The time simply wasn't right for her and Max.

His priority was his business. And hers was her daughter. When Kaylee was older and could understand more, then Jane might try dating again. But now, it wasn't working. Kaylee had formed such a strong attachment, and so quickly… Jane had made a mistake, and it was time to undo it. Clearly she wasn't ready for a relationship. She needed to be just Jane for a while, so she could be sure she wasn't grabbing on to the first available man because she wanted security, as she'd done with Scott.

Max didn't represent security anyway. He'd told her flat out not to count on commitment from him. He'd just escaped from a job and a family that were constricting him. Why would he jump into another situation where he would feel obligated to put other people's needs ahead of his own?

Anyway, his last serious relationship had ended when the woman wanted permanence and Max didn't.

An emphatic knock at her door made her drop a frying pan she was about to pack, which barely missed her foot. She whirled around and saw a very anxious face peering through the window.

Max. Oh dear. She wasn't ready to face him, but he'd caught her playing hooky from work, so she hurried to unlock the hatch and let him in.

At first he just stood there, and they stared at each other mutely. The bewildered look on his face made her heart ache, and she wanted to shrink away from it.

Surely when she explained, he would understand.

"Come in, Max," she finally managed.

He walked down the three steps, all the while taking in her, the salon, the half-filled boxes and bubble wrap. "You're moving?"

She wanted to touch him, to make some connection with him, but the urge was inappropriate just now. "Well, yes."

He stared at her and she looked away. How in the world was she going to explain this to him?

"Did something go wrong with your divorce settlement? I swear, if Scott swindled you—"

"No, it has nothing to do with him."

"Then what's going on? You said this morning you needed to talk to me. So talk."

"I was upset, and your brother was visiting and I wasn't sure if I could hold it together in front of him. I know it's important to you to make a good impression on Eddie—"

"To hell with Eddie. Why are you upset? If you got a better job offer, why didn't you tell me? I know I'm the one who said I didn't want to hold you back, but we can talk about a raise—"

"What? Max, I would never walk out because I got a better job offer."

"Are you walking out, though?"

She hesitated, not wanting to just blurt it out this way. If there was any way she could stay on… "I'll stay until you find someone to replace me. I won't leave you in the lurch, I promise."

"Jane, you better tell me what's going on."

She was perilously close to losing it again. It would be so much better if she could explain things calmly and rationally. But her emotions were too close to the surface, and Max was agitated.

Max squeezed the bridge of his nose. "Is it another man? Oh, God, you're not going back to Scott, are you?"

"Max! That you could even think I would do that—"
She almost growled in frustration, turning away and
stomping to the kitchen to continue her packing. He *had*
to know her better than that.

She chucked a couple more pans into the box, not
even bothering to cushion them with paper. They made
loud, satisfying clunks as they hit. But out of the corner
of her eye, she also watched Max.

He walked to one of the chairs, moved a half-filled
box to the floor, and sat down. Then he reached for a
roll of brown packing tape, ripped off a few inches, and
slapped it over his mouth.

The gesture brought a smile to her face, and her
anger evaporated. In that moment she realized she loved
him. Loved him and was in love with him. A man who
could admit he was wrong, one with a sense of humor
even in a crisis—how often did she run across one of
those?

But her being in love wasn't enough fix everything.

Jane abandoned her packing and cleared a place for
herself on the coffee table across from him. They were
close, but not touching.

"The problem is Kaylee."

Max's eyes filled with panic, and he ripped the tape
off his mouth. "Oh, God, she's not sick, is she?"

"No. But this morning, after she saw us…well, she's
ready for you to move in permanently and be her
daddy."

Jane expected some sort of panic reaction from Max,
but instead his face softened. "Oh."

"I tried to explain the situation, but you can't reason with an almost-four-year-old."

"What happened? Did she throw a tantrum or what?"

"I could have handled that. But it was worse. She was…bereft. That's the only word I can use to explain it. She cried, but quietly. It was the worst thing I've ever witnessed, worse than seeing her fall and scrape her knee. Even worse than watching Scott walk away from her in that restaurant like she meant nothing to him."

Max looked almost bereft himself. "We're breaking up?"

"I don't want to, believe me. But—"

"So is the answer that you just won't have a social life?"

"I can have a social life," she argued.

"Sure. Of course. And maybe you can date men that Kaylee doesn't like so well, ones who ignore her and consider her a pest, so she won't get attached."

"Max, please. You're not making this any easier."

"I don't intend to make it easy. I intend to make it damn difficult for you to walk out of my life. Have you really thought about what you're doing?"

"I've thought of nothing else. I don't see any other choice."

Max stood up and headed for the door. But he didn't leave. He opened the hatch, took a couple of deep breaths. Jane just sat there helplessly.

Finally he closed the hatch and turned to face her again. "Look, if you really feel you don't want to see me outside of work, that's one thing, but you don't have to leave the Remington Agency. I promised you our seeing each other wouldn't interfere with your job, and it won't."

"Yes, it will," she said, her voice ringing with resignation. "You know it will. I don't think I could see you day in and day out and just pretend to be friends. We can't go backward."

Jane's eyes filled with tears, and she buried her face in her hands.

Max closed the distance between them with two steps, and she prayed he wouldn't try to comfort her. But apparently comfort wasn't what he had in mind.

"Jane Selwyn, I never took you for a quitter. One of the reasons I hired you was because of your gumption. The way you attack problems and just go for what you want—it's a rare quality. It's also one of the reasons I fell in love with you."

Jane's world tilted on its axis for a brief moment. She was so startled her tears stopped abruptly and she peeked through her fingers up at Max. Had he really just said what she thought he said?

But yes, she could see it there in his eyes, the love shining through.

He sat back down in the chair across from her. "There's an easy solution to this whole thing, and I can't believe you didn't see it. We'll get married."

"What?"

"It's perfect. Kaylee wants me to be her daddy, I'll be her daddy."

"But…but…" *Oh, my God.* Jane sprang up from her

chair. She needed to move, to pace, but every direction she stepped there was another box or piece of furniture. Boat cabins were no good for pacing.

"You have a problem with this?" he asked, as if he'd just brought her a coffee with too much cream rather than confidently declaring they should spend the rest of their lives together.

"You can't just go around marrying someone because their kid wants you as a daddy!" she exploded. "There are a million reasons we can't get married. I just got divorced. You're my boss. You're a confirmed bachelor—"

"Who says?"

"You. At the Hotel Alexander. You said you didn't like dating single moms angling for marriage. Then you said it again, after we made love the first time. You told me you weren't ready to settle down."

"I was in denial. I was scared by how deeply I was starting to care for you. None of it was true."

"But, Max…marriage? What about all those women?"

He looked puzzled. "What women?"

"Your little black book is bulging with them. You're going to give that up?"

He reached into his jacket, extracting the worn leather address book. "This? You want to know how much all those other women mean to me? I'll show you." He got up and headed outdoors.

Jane followed. "Max, what are you doing?"

He walked all the way to the *Princess II*'s stern, then wound up like a baseball pitcher and hurled the book into the bay.

"Max! You had business contacts in there, too."

He turned and smiled at her as if he didn't have a care in the world. "The important ones are on computer." But then he turned serious. "There would be only one reason in the world why we shouldn't get married, and that's if you don't love me. Do you love me, Jane?"

She nodded, afraid to speak.

"Then, seriously, will you marry me? 'Cause I'm not kidding around here. We are good together. All of us— you, me, Kaylee. I'll try to be the best husband and father I know how to be. And since I know you don't like the idea of marrying the boss, I have a solution for that, too."

"You're firing me?"

Max slapped a hand to his forehead. "Jane, for God's sake, I'm not going to fire you. I actually came over here with a very different proposal in mind, a business proposal. I want to make you a partner in the agency. An equal, 50-50 partner. I want to change the name to Remington & Selwyn. You've already invested a significant amount of money in the— Oh."

Jane was suddenly dizzy, and she sank onto one of the padded benches. "What?"

"I just realized where the money came from. You sold your boat. Damn it, Jane, you just march right back in there and unpack. We'll buy it back."

"With what? Max, it's a done deal. I wanted to sell the *Princess II.* I believe in you and the Remington Agency. It was a sound investment."

Finally he smiled at her. "See, you're already thinking

like a partner. You've been functioning like one almost since the beginning. You're involved in decision-making and key meetings. Frankly, I'm not sure we can survive without you. So what do you think?"

Jane pursed her lips, appearing to give it serious thought. "I think it would be too expensive to change the name of the agency. That would mean a new logo, new legal papers to file, all new stationery…"

Max looked at her quizzically.

"I think," Jane continued, "it would just be easier if I changed my name to Remington."

Max smiled again, like the sun coming out from behind a cloud. "Cheeky. That's what I thought of you the day you tried to guilt me into a job. Cheeky girl." But when he swept her into his arms, there was nothing amusing about his kiss. He kissed her long and hard until Jane was so limp she could have melted over the side of the boat.

When they were both in danger of fainting from oxygen deprivation, he pulled back just enough so he could look her in the eye. "I want to hear you say it."

She knew immediately what he meant. "I love you, Max, and I enthusiastically accept all proposals."

Epilogue

"Mommy!" Kaylee had apparently seen their car coming, because she bolted out the front door of the Sunsetter B and B before Jane and Max could reach the front porch.

Jane dropped her purse and leaned down to scoop up her little girl, hugging her and covering her face with kisses. Her honeymoon with Max—all of five days—was the longest she and Kaylee had ever been separated.

"Oof, I think you grew while we were gone!" Jane said as she set Kaylee down. "I guess Aunt Sara hasn't let you miss any meals."

But Kaylee wasn't listening. Her eyes were for Max, and his were for her. He picked her up and swung her into the air. "Oh, my gosh, am I happy to see you." He hugged her, too, and Kaylee threw her arms around him with abandon. The look of pure bliss on the little girl's face did Jane a world of good.

Given Kaylee's attachment issues, Jane had worried about how she would fare with both her mother and Max gone for five days. But Sara, who had happily agreed to care for Kaylee during the honeymoon, had reported that she handled it fine. A daily call from Jane and Max had reassured Kaylee that she hadn't been abandoned.

Sara met them at the door, so eager to hug them that she barely let them inside. "You all look great! How was Jamaica? I've always wanted to go there. Reece, let's go there next vacation."

Reece was right behind her, also with a hug for Jane and a hearty handshake and thorough shoulder-pounding for Max that ended in one of those quick, self-conscious guy hugs.

"Step aside, the party can start now," came a voice from behind Jane.

She whirled around and found Cooper and Allie right behind her. "Hey, what's going on?"

"Just a little gathering," Sara said innocently. "Since you guys wouldn't let me throw you a big wedding, I did the next best thing. A party. You know how I love parties."

"Oh, Sara." Jane hugged her friend again.

Others soon arrived—Eddie and his wife, Rhonda; Carol and her new beau, Reggie; friends, neighbors and people Jane and Max had never even met—they all showed up to toast the newlyweds and enjoy Sara's fabulous buffet.

Minutes earlier, Jane had been exhausted from traveling and was looking forward to retreating with her newly reengineered family to her cozy beach house. She and Max had bought the house that Kaylee had so loved when she and Jane were looking for a place to live, and after a bit of sprucing up, it would be everything a home should be.

But she was touched by her friends' efforts on her part, and her fatigue lifted as she sampled everything on the buffet and celebrated her marriage with her friends. Who would have guessed that in a few short months she would go from divorced, destitute and jobless to having so much!

Max had healed her broken heart, but he'd healed her spirit, too, and allowed her to blossom into the person she was meant to be. Kaylee was also thriving now that she had the fatherly love she had so desperately needed.

Jane exchanged a look with Max across the room and her heart swelled with the love she saw in his eyes. She'd caught a good one this time.

Max couldn't help grinning as he returned his attention to Reece, who was excited about the 401k plans he'd set up for all of the Remington Agency's employees.

"Reece," Sara said sternly as she breezed past with a tray of crab cakes. "That doesn't sound like party talk."

"Sorry." He looked suitably chastised, but when she left, he grinned. "She has eyes in the back of her head and supersonic hearing."

Cooper joined them and announced in a conspiratorial whisper, "Meet me on the patio in five minutes. Don't let anyone follow you."

Reece rolled his eyes, but five minutes later the three cousins assembled on the back patio, where a sharp November north wind kept everyone else away.

"I've been saving this bottle for when the last of us fell. Frankly, I thought it would be years before I dragged it out." He produced a bottle of aged Scotch from a blue velvet bag. Three glasses sat on the patio table, ready to be filled.

"I don't know why you all thought I was so antimarriage," Max said as he picked up his glass.

"Oh, only that you said just about every day you'd never get married," Reece replied.

"A long time ago, when I was young and stupid. I never said that once since I met Jane."

"No quibbling," Cooper said as he filled his own glass. "I want you to turn your mind back to the last time we had a toast like this."

"At your house," Reece recalled. "Right before you got married to Allie."

"Right. And do you remember what we said?"

"As I recall," Max said, "we were all depressed because it was the end of an era. The split-up of the Three Musketeers."

Cooper nodded in agreement. "But it wasn't the end of anything. It was the beginning of a new era. I don't think any of us had any idea how radically our lives would change when we took an innocent trip to Texas to check out the fishing boat Uncle Johnny left to us."

"Amen to that," Reece said.

"So I think we should drink to Uncle Johnny Remington. He lived life on his terms. And when he died, he gave us all a great gift. He encouraged us to live our lives on our own terms. Now we all get along better with the family than we ever did when we worked at Remington Industries."

"It's all turned out better than I expected," Max said as he raised his glass. "Even my parents are speaking to me again. A toast to Johnny."

"To Johnny," the others echoed.

"And to our beautiful, talented and loving wives," Reece added. "Without whom we would all be miserable and crabby."

"Hear, hear," Max and Cooper agreed.

Max thought a bit before he offered his own toast. But finally he knew exactly what should be said. He raised his glass. "To the new generation of Remingtons. Kaylee and all the as-yet-unnamed children we'll have, to the great things they'll accomplish and the adventures they'll have. Maybe we'll be wise enough as fathers to let them lead their own lives."

Reece and Cooper nodded and raised their glasses again.

Cooper grinned. "To…what he said."

The toasts continued until they no longer felt the cold wind. But Scotch wasn't the only thing heating Max up. All he had to do was think about Jane and Kaylee, and the fire in his heart burned bright and warm.

* * * * *

Celebrate 60 years of pure reading pleasure
with Harlequin®!

Step back in time and enjoy a sneak preview of an
exciting anthology from Harlequin® Historical with
THE DIAMONDS OF WELBOURNE MANOR

This compelling anthology features three stories
about the outrageous Fitzmanning sisters. Meet
Annalise, who is never at a loss for words… But
that can change with an unexpected encounter in
the forest.

Available May 2009
from Harlequin® Historical.

"I'm the illegitimate daughter of notoriously scandalous parents, Mr. Milford. Candidates for my hand are unlikely to be lining up at the gates."

"Don't be so quick to discount your charms, my dear. Or the charm of your substantial dowry. Or even your brothers' influence. There are as many reasons to marry as there are marriages."

Annalise snorted. "Oh, yes. Perhaps I shall marry for dynastic reasons, or perhaps for property or influence. After all, a loveless, practical marriage worked out so well for my mother."

"Well, you've routed me on that one. I can think of no suitable rejoinder." Ned rose to his feet and extended his hand. "And since that is the case, let me be the first to wish you a long and happy spinsterhood."

Her mouth gaped open. And then she laughed.

And he froze.

This was the first time, Ned realized. The first time he'd seen her eyes light up and her mouth curl. The first time he'd witnessed her features melded together in glorious accord to produce exquisite beauty.

Unbelievable what a change came over her face. Unheard of what effect her throaty, rasping laughter had on his body. It pounded a beat upon his ear, quickly taken up by his pulse. It echoed through him, finally residing in his stirring nether regions.

So easily she did it, awakened these sensations within him—without any apparent effort at all. And she had called him potentially dangerous? Clearly the intelligent thing for him to do would be to steer clear, to leave her to the tender ministrations of Lord Peter Blackthorne.

"You were right." She smiled up at him as she took his hand and climbed to her feet. "I do feel better."

Ah, well. When had he ever chosen the intelligent path?

He did not relinquish her hand. He used it to pull her in, close enough that he could feel the warmth of her. "At the risk of repeating Lord Peter's mistake and anticipating too much—may I ask if you'll be my partner in battledore tomorrow?"

Her smiled dimmed. Her breath came a little faster. His own had gone shallow, as if he'd just run a race—and lost. He ran his gaze over the appealing lift of her brow and the curious angle of her chin. His index finger twitched.

"I should like that," she said.

His finger trembled again and he lifted it, traced the pink and tender shell of her ear, the unique sweep of her jaw. Her pulse leaped beneath her skin, triggering his own. Slowly he tilted her chin up, waiting for her to object, to step back, to slap his hand away.

She did none of those eminently sensible things. Which left him free to do the entirely impractical thing.

Baby soft, the skin of her lips. Her whole body trembled when he touched her there.

He leaned in. Her eyes closed, even as she stood straight against him, strung as tight as a bow. He pressed his mouth to hers. It was a soft kiss, sweet and chaste. And yet he was hot and hard and as ready as he'd ever been in his life.

She drew back a little. Sighed. Their breath mingled a moment before she slowly backed away.

"Oh," she breathed. Her dark eyes were full of wonder and something that looked like fear. He took a step toward her, but she only shook her head. His outstretched hand fell to his side as she turned to disappear into the wood. This was the first time, Ned realized. The first time, since he'd come to the house party at Welbourne Manor, that he'd seen her eyes light up.

* * * * *

*Follow Ned and Annalise's story in May 2009 in
THE DIAMONDS OF WELBOURNE MANOR
Available May 2009 from Harlequin® Historical*

Available in the series romance section, or in the historical romance section, wherever books are sold.

**We'll be spotlighting a different series
every month throughout 2009
to celebrate our 60th anniversary.**

Look for Harlequin® Historical in May!

Celebrations begin with
a sumptuous Regency house party!

Join three scandalous sisters in

**THE DIAMONDS OF
WELBOURNE MANOR**

Glittering, scintillating, sensual fun
by Diane Gaston, Deb Marlowe
and Amanda McCabe.

**60 years of Harlequin,
600 years of romance
in Harlequin Historical!**

You're invited to join our Tell Harlequin Reader Panel!

By joining our new reader panel you will:

- Receive Harlequin® books—they are FREE and yours to keep with no obligation to purchase anything!
- Participate in fun online surveys
- Exchange opinions and ideas with women just like you
- Have a say in our new book ideas and help us publish the best in women's fiction

In addition, you will have a chance to win great prizes and receive special gifts! See Web site for details. Some conditions apply. Space is limited.

To join, visit us at

www.TellHarlequin.com.

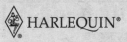
HARLEQUIN®

American ★ Romance®

LAURA MARIE ALTOM
The Marine's Babies

Men Made in America

Captain Jace Monroe is everything a Marine
should be—strong, brave and honorable. He's also
an instant father of twin baby girls he never knew
existed! Life gets even more complicated when he
finds himself attracted to Emma Stewart, his new
nanny. But can this sexy, fun-loving bachelor do
the right thing and become a family man?
Emma and the babies are counting on it!

Available in May
wherever books are sold.

LOVE, HOME & HAPPINESS

REQUEST YOUR FREE BOOKS!

2 FREE NOVELS PLUS 2
FREE GIFTS!

Love, Home & Happiness!

Our

ON BOARD

miniseries has grown!

Now you can share in even more
tears and triumphs as
Harlequin Romance® brings you
a month full of

Pregnancy and Proposals,
Miracles and Marriage!

*Available in May
wherever books are sold.*

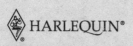

COMING NEXT MONTH
Available May 12, 2009

#1257 THE MARINE'S BABIES by Laura Marie Altom
Men Made in America

Captain Jace Monroe is everything a marine should be—strong, brave and honorable. He's also an instant father of twin baby girls he didn't know existed! Life gets even more complicated when he finds himself attracted to Emma Stewart, his new nanny. But can this sexy, fun-loving bachelor do the right thing and become a family man? Emma and the baby brigade are counting on it!

#1258 ONCE A HERO by Lisa Childs
Citizen's Police Academy

Taking a bullet meant for someone else made Kent Terlecki a hero in the eyes of his fellow detectives. But Erin Powell doesn't see the brave cop behind the badge—just a man who put her brother in jail. Then the justice-seeking reporter enrolls in the Lakewood Citizen's Police Academy, looking for some answers…and finding the truth about an incredible man.

#1259 THE MAN MOST LIKELY by Cindi Myers

Bryan Perry is gorgeous and charismatic—the type of guy that Angela Krisova avoids. The full-figured gal has been jilted before. With her own successful business and fun social life, who needs to stir up trouble? So it's confusing when suddenly Bryan seems bent on pursuing *her*. Could this most unlikely of men be the one to win her heart?

#1260 HER VERY OWN FAMILY by Trish Milburn

Audrey York is running from a scandalous past and is determined to find peace in Willow Glen, Tennessee. Instead she finds Brady Witt, who is suspicious of her sudden interest in his widowed father. Audrey doesn't want her past to jeopardize Brady's and his dad's reputations, but she can't help hoping for what she's always wanted—a family of her own.

www.eHarlequin.com